PAPER CUTS

by

Bob Biderman

LONDON
VICTOR GOLLANCZ LTD
1990

First published in Great Britain 1990
by Victor Gollancz Ltd,
14 Henrietta Street, London WC2E 8QJ

British Library Cataloguing in Publication Data
Biderman, Bob
   Paper cuts.
   I. Title
   813.54 [F]

   ISBN 0-575-04912-X

Typeset by CentraCet, Cambridge
Printed in Great Britain by St Edmunsbury Press Ltd
Bury St Edmunds, Suffolk

In memory of Mike and Norma

Chapter *1*

It wasn't his imagination. The house actually smiled at him as he trudged down the pebble drive toward the wood-shingled facade with its three windows shaped like belly-up half moons. Set back in a grove of eucalyptus trees some hundred yards from the steep, windy road that led from the coastal flatlands to the lush Tiburon hills, and perched on the edge of a rocky cliff, the far side of the house looked out onto an expanse of blue where sky met sea in a celebration of celestial grandeur that only moneyed Californians and astronauts could truly call their own.

Following a stone path that worked its way around the smiling side to the front that faced the spectacular view, he reached the entrance and pressed the buttoned nose of a brass lion built into the woodwork of the door. The buzzer set off a series of electronic chimes that sounded the theme song from a Hollywood film.

Joseph stared at the lion's nose in wonder.

The door opened as he was about to press the nose for an encore. A pair of sparkling black eyes set in a pretty Oriental face greeted him.

"Mr Radkin?" she said in a voice that was as bright as her sleek black hair.

He looked down at her tiny figure dressed only in a silky robe that was the same color as the hair that fell lightly on her shoulders. If it wasn't that she had addressed him by name, he would have wondered whether he had come to the right place.

"Please to follow me," she said, bowing her head and dipping slightly at the knees. The bow was as brief and easy as a wink.

When she raised her head and her eyes met his again, he could see that they were laughing.

She led him into an enormous room underneath a dome. A semicircular couch of glove-soft leather echoed the shape above. Fitted into the arc of the couch, with about three feet of legroom between, was a gigantic rounded coffee table of polished mahogany. The center of the couch faced a black marble fireplace with a lion's head mantelpiece that looked like the twin of the one on the door.

"What happens when you press that one's nose?" He glanced up at the ceiling. "The dome opens and we fly out into space?"

Her head tilted slightly to one side. She seemed amused, but it was hard to say. "I sorry. I not speak English very good."

"Don't worry about it," he said. "No one does anymore."

Her eyes laughed again as she said, "A moment, please." And then she tripped quietly out, leaving him alone in the vastness of the room.

Joseph sat down on the luxurious couch, allowing the richness of the leather to encompass him. A cathedral window to the right of the fireplace let in a brilliant beam of heavenly light of such perfection that a man of god might have given his soul to the devil if only it could have been replicated in his church.

"Mr Radkin?"

It was a deep voice. Resonant. But then, he thought, what in this place wouldn't be?

He turned his head past the blinding light toward the voice that had come from the direction of the circular stairs which wound like a helix from the balcony above.

A silhouette of a figure was bounding down. He heard a voice say, "Please, don't get up."

He got up anyhow.

Joseph felt the energy of his presence before he actually saw the man. "I'm very happy you could come." The man stuck out his hand.

What Joseph finally saw was dressed in a white terry-cloth robe that matched the coils of flaxen hair atop his head. His face was square—or most likely had been before his chin had started to sag. He had an aquiline nose and heavy brows over

8

deep-set eyes which seemed to be busily studying the image in front of them. It was a straightforward look from a well-used face. And if he had to sum it up, Joseph probably would have guessed its owner was pretty satisfied, even though his time was almost up. But, then again, with such an expensive view and nothing blocking the way, why wouldn't he be satisfied? Joseph asked himself as he reached out and gave the proffered hand a shake.

So this was Saunders, Joseph thought. The man who helped bankroll *Investigations Magazine*. West's silent partner—whatever that meant. Fairy godfather or entrepreneur? Surely there couldn't have been much money in it—though Joseph hadn't been privy to their profit sheet. As long as he got his check on time it was all right by him.

Saunders motioned to the crevice Joseph's body had made in the couch. "Go ahead. Sit back down. Tell Yoko what you want to drink."

He hadn't noticed her come back in. She walked like a cat. A very quiet and contented Siamese. She stood next to Saunders, smiling silently. She was about half his height and different in most every way. The contrast was striking—accentuated by their robes. Then he remembered the wire service story that had been meant for the fashion editor but had been put in his box by mistake. White on black was in this year. Or was it black on white?

"Orange juice," said Joseph.

"OJ for you, too, William?" she asked, looking up at Saunders with her playful eyes.

Joseph glanced down and noticed that her tiny feet were naked. Her child-like toes were painted the brightest red he'd ever seen. And one of them was rubbing, seductively, up against Saunders' Achilles tendon—or so it seemed.

If Saunders felt anything, he didn't show it. "OJ all around," he said, rubbing his hands together. "Loaded with vitamin C. Keeps you vigorous! Right, Radkin?

"I wouldn't know," said Joseph. "I just have a hell of a hangover . . ."

"Try pure grain alcohol next time," he said. "It's the additives that get you."

"I'll keep it in mind," Joseph replied. He looked over to where Yoko had been. She had disappeared again. Off to get the orange juice most likely.

Saunders had moved to the cathedral window and was looking out. "Terrific view, isn't it?" he said, turning around and pointing a finger toward the glass.

Joseph crossed his legs and rubbed a painful knee that had just started acting up again. "Is that why you asked me over? To appreciate the view?" He said that to himself. To Saunders he said, "Not bad."

"Not bad?" Even through the blinding light he could see him smile. "I thought you were our star investigative journalist, Radkin. Surely you could think of more exciting phraseology . . ."

"I save the hyperbole for my copy. Don't want to use it up too fast."

The orange juice came in tall crystal glasses set on a black lacquered tray. It was fresh-squeezed. Joseph could tell by all the little seeds floating on the top.

"Let's take these out on the veranda," said Saunders, leading the way to a sliding glass door at the far side of the room.

Joseph got up and followed, somewhat reluctantly as he was beginning to enjoy the soft leather couch. On the other hand, with a salary like his, it was better not to get used to the feel of luxury.

The deck was made of redwood. The long side faced the hills; the short side faced the sea. He could have guessed there would have been a hot tub. But he wouldn't have pictured one so large and that spewed out so much steam.

"What did West tell you?" asked Saunders as they sat down at a large chrome and glass table under an umbrella that kept out the sun.

"He said that he was putting me on sabbatical and that I was to take my instructions from you for a couple of weeks." Joseph took a sip of his orange juice and then looked Saunders squarely in the eye. "He said you'd tell me what it was all about. But he didn't seem pleased."

"Look up there," said Saunders, turning toward the hills. "You know what those are?" He pointed to the trees.

"Eucalyptus. Polly—my wife—collects the leaves and stuffs them into old socks. The odor is supposed to keep away the fleas."

"They're not native to California, you know," said Saunders. "Brought here some sixty or seventy years ago by people with small minds and big ideas. Eucalyptus grows remarkably fast, ten times faster than your ordinary evergreen. In Australia they have a species *E. regnans*, the giant eucalyptus, that reaches a height of three hundred feet with a twenty-five-foot girth. It yields a hardwood, very strong, used in shipbuilding."

"You'd think that if they were used for shipbuilding they'd have been cut down years ago," said Joseph, raising his glass to the trees.

"That's right. And they would have been, too—except the idiots who brought them over took the wrong species. They brought over *E. globulus*, the blue gum. Commercially, the wood was worthless."

"Lucky for your view," said Joseph.

"Yes. Up until now . . ."

"I thought you said the wood was worthless."

"It was. However, recently they've been using them in Brazil to make paper. Eucalyptus wood is very white, you see. Much whiter than your ordinary wood. By using eucalyptus the paper companies can circumvent the bleaching process . . ."

"That's very interesting," said Joseph. "Bits of trivia like that can work their way nicely into stories for wildlife magazines."

"Bleaching, in case you haven't been reading the press, is what's causing the build-up of dioxin in our rivers and streams."

"And acid rain is causing the leaching of heavy metals into our ground waters," said Joseph, somewhat impatiently. "I do read the papers, Mr Saunders. And I know we haven't been treating the earth too kindly. But if all this has anything to do with the story you'd like me to write, I'd remind you that the rivers and lakes are Michael's territory. He's a great environmental reporter. I'm more at home on the city beat. In fact, flowers make me sneeze."

"Don't worry," said Saunders, letting out a laugh. "I'm not

about to issue you a knapsack and an axe." Then, looking at Joseph more seriously, he said, "And you're perfectly free to refuse my offer—it won't be held against you."

"I'll bet!" Joseph said to himself.

"But hear me out," Saunders continued. "And keep in mind that whoever takes on this assignment will be paid very well." He seemed to be studying Joseph's face again. "You're not averse to money, are you?"

"I suppose it depends on where it comes from and what I do to get it," Joseph replied.

"Money comes from paper. There's a bit of eighteenth-century doggerel which goes: 'Rags make paper, paper makes money, money makes banks, banks make loans, loans make beggars, beggars make rags.' So you see, it's all a neat and tidy little circle."

"I thought it was trees that make paper."

"In the eighteenth century it was rags. Trees have only been used for a hundred years or so."

"That's comforting," said Joseph. Then he looked at Saunders, suspiciously. "You don't want me to do a story about trees, I hope."

"Only in a roundabout way," Saunders replied. He hesitated a moment, then he said, "I have a friend—an old, dear friend—who seems to be in trouble . . ."

"What kind of trouble?" He knew he shouldn't have asked. But it was instinctual.

"I'm not exactly sure. He's a professor out at Meade College."

"That's in Oregon, isn't it?"

"Yes, Portland."

"What's his field?"

"Earth sciences, I think they call it. Anyway, he's very active in the environmental movement. Working to clean up the Columbia River—things like that. Seems one of the paper companies is trying to set up a new pulp mill. He's been one of the main people fighting to deny them certification."

"Because of the bleaching process, I take it."

"Yes. The process produces a number of chlorohydrate

effluents, one of which is dioxin—supposedly the most toxic chemical known to man."

"And they dump it in the river?"

"Minute quantities, of course. It's only recently that they've been able to assess the damage. It builds up, you see. In the tissues and the liver. Becomes part of the food chain . . ."

"I understand," said Joseph. "You want a story on the perils of the paper industry. But what's so urgent?"

Saunders turned in his chair and gazed out at the other magnificent view, where the sky met the sea. "I've been following your work, Radkin. I've seen how you've been able to make the big story out of the small."

"It depends on how big and how small you're talking about. I usually have something more to go on."

Saunders turned back around and looked at Joseph. "Oregon is our economic hinterland, Radkin. It's brimming with nature. But it's also our last untrammeled wilderness, besides Alaska. What happens there in the next few years may truly determine the fate of our nation."

"That might be going a little far."

"I don't think so," said Saunders. "Anyway, the situation in Oregon is growing dangerous. Battle lines have been drawn . . ."

"Between who and whom?"

"The environmentalists and the logging interests. Last week a logger was killed . . ."

"Shot?"

Saunders shook his head. "No. An environmental terrorist spiked a tree. That's a tactic some of those loonies use to try and stop the lumberjacks. They nail a railroad spike into the trunk so deep you can't see it. When the chainsaw hits it, the chain shatters. The backlash can kill you. It usually doesn't. In this case it did."

"I thought you were on those tree savers' side."

Saunders swallowed the last of his drink and then pushed his glass away. He seemed somewhat perturbed. "I agree with their objective, but not their methods."

That's very liberal of you, Joseph thought.

"Anyway, it came at a terrible time. Tempers are at the

13

flashpoint now. And it's all focused around the permit battle for the new pulp mill. The loggers want it. The environmentalists don't."

Joseph rubbed his knee again. Just the thought of pulp mills made it hurt.

Saunders was staring at him without blinking his eyes. "So? What do you say?"

"Frankly—if you want to know the honest truth—it's probably front page stuff in Oregon, page four stuff in California and might make page thirteen in New York if you're lucky."

"You're missing the point, Radkin," Saunders said, getting up from his chair and walking over to the rail. He looked up at the eucalyptus forest. "This is a private bit of research I want you to do for me. I want you to find out what you can about the events surrounding the McCullough Paper Company's permit application for their new pulp mill. And I want it by the end of the week. In fact, I want you to fax a copy to me by midnight, Friday."

"I don't get it," said Joseph. "Why?"

"I have my reasons," he said.

Saunders then turned around and made a sign toward the sliding door. A moment later, Yoko came out and handed him a briefcase. She seemed to hover by his side as he placed the briefcase on the deck table, opened it up and took out an envelope which he handed to Joseph.

"All you need to know is in here. It contains the names of a couple of people you should contact. I've arranged for a reporter on the Portland daily to assist you. There's also an airline ticket . . ."

"An airline ticket?"

"Alaska Airlines. The flight leaves 9.00 p.m. Tonight."

Joseph stared at him incredulously.

"There's a check enclosed in the sum of two thousand dollars. For expenses. You'll receive another check for three thousand dollars at the completion of your assignment."

"For one week's work?"

"For one week's work."

Joseph glanced at Yoko. She was full of smiles.

"Is that payment on approval?"

"I have full confidence in your investigatory skills," said Saunders. "As long as you fax me your copy by midnight, Friday, you'll receive the second check when you return."

Yoko had left the table and was walking down the length of redwood deck toward the hot tub. Out of the corner of his eye, Joseph saw her loosen the tie cord of her robe and let it fall from her shoulders to the ground. Her naked body seemed to glow in the sunlight as she slid into the steamy waters.

Taking the envelope, Joseph put it in his pocket.

"Come William!" she called. Her voice reminded him of a sparrow. He turned to look. Her face was half hidden by the vapors. But he could see her dainty hand held out.

He turned back to Saunders and saw him wink.

"OK?" he said.

"I wouldn't want to hold you up," Joseph replied. "I'll see you in a week." Time enough, he thought, for Saunders to bathe and dry himself out.

Chapter 2

He had packed his valise with basic stuff—shirts, socks, underwear, an extra pair of trousers. His worksuit, a brown tweed jacket with coordinated slacks, was what he had on. There was a small hole in the slacks from a cigarette ember which had landed there during a melee with an excitable congressman who took exception to an article relating him to some funny business regarding the oil industry, supertankers and petroleum spills. And the buttons of the jacket were somewhat out of line—a reminder of when an angry cop who had just been convicted of tampering with vital evidence in a murder case that linked a prominent real estate developer and a child pornography ring grabbed him by the lapel and shook him so hard that the buttons had snapped off.

Polly had once gotten so fed up with his outfit that she tried putting the jacket and trousers in a bundle she had made up for the Salvation Army. He had saved them in the nick of time. After several days of his hostile looks and grunted remarks reminding her that these were wounds of honor, she had made her peace with his obsession. Where clothing was concerned, they lived in a world apart.

"I still don't understand what this is all about." Polly was standing beside him in the bedroom watching him close his battered valise.

He clicked the case shut, straightened himself up and then reached into the pocket of his jacket. He pulled out the check and handed it to her. "You can deposit this in our account. What's the balance?" he asked.

"Minus fifty," she replied. Her eyes scanned the numerals

on the slip of paper. She let out a low whistle. "Two thousand smackers!" She looked at him. "For expenses?"

"Well the mortgage is an expense, isn't it?"

"And he's paying you three thousand besides?"

"Yeah."

"Who do you have to kill?"

"I don't know yet." He tightened the belt around the valise. "Did you phone for a cab?"

"It'll be here any minute." She came up close and put her arms around him with her hands down low enough to caress his cheeks. He recognized the look in her eye. "Care for a little huggle before you go?"

Smiling, he drew her closer still. "I wouldn't mind."

He was kissing her mouth and working his way slowly across to nibble her ear when he sensed something whizz by. It hovered momentarily in the air above and then nose-dived— plonk!—onto his head.

There was a tittering of tiny voices by the door. He glanced over just in time to see little feet scurrying away.

She shrugged her shoulders and looked at him apologetically. "I forgot about the twins. They wanted to say goodbye."

On the floor, right beside them, lay the remains of a paper airplane.

"I hope that's not mine," she heard him say.

His, in fact, was a twin-engine job bound for Anchorage with stops in Portland and Seattle. It wasn't paper, but whatever it was didn't seem to be holding up too well in the storm. Neither was Joseph's stomach.

It was after his second trip to the john that the man in the aisle seat introduced himself: "Russ Armstrong," he said, sticking out a hand that was as white and clammy as Joseph's forehead. "You look pretty bad. Probably don't fly much, I bet. Me, I got enough frequent flyer credits to take me up to Mars and back. These little blows don't bother me none. Used to, when I was still wet behind the ears. Now I can eat raw oysters and fly through a hurricane without bringin' 'em up.

Care to change seats? From the looks of things, seems to me you might need the pork house again."

Joseph gratefully changed seats with him, spreading his legs out into the aisle which seemed to take the pressure off his groaning abdomen.

"It's the currents, see," the man continued, as if his act of sacrifice made Joseph duty-bound to withstand what was becoming a verbal torrent. "Once you reach the Siskiyous you get caught up in a mass of supersaturated air. If you was driving, you'd probably be hung up in fog just about the time you hit the Oregon border. It's what happens when the cold wet air of the north hits the warm air from the south. Up here the two of them battle it out, punching and shaking and squeezing until the water's all wrung out. Down below you get the rain. A constant drip, drip, drip. That's Oregon. Drip, drip, drip. The ducks love it here, I'll tell you. But even they gotta wear galoshes."

He looked over at Joseph. Armstrong's bald, round face was cherry bright. He nudged his elbow into Joseph's ribs. "You ever see a duck in galoshes?" He rolled up the sleeve of his jacket and showed him his cuff-links. Their face wore the image of a grinning duck in wellingtons. "Oregon State Mutual gave them to me for saving them two million bucks on a case. Mighty generous of them, wouldn't you say?"

"Excuse me," Joseph said, getting up and heading toward the lavatories once again.

He stayed on the toilet an awfully long time. The air was smoother when he finally came out.

Stopping for a drink of water before going back to his seat, he noticed that Armstrong had gotten up to retrieve his briefcase from the overhead baggage. By the time Joseph had arrived back at his place, Armstrong was seated again and was reading a business magazine.

He looked up as Joseph sat down. "Feel better? Should be smooth sailing now," he said. "Just a half hour more to Portland. What hotel are you staying at, by the way?"

"How did you know I was going to Portland?" asked Joseph. He looked at the bald-headed man, suspiciously.

"Ain't no mystery, pal. I was looking for my appointment

book. Seems it decided to take a vacation from me. I noticed your valise in the luggage compartment above. Joseph Radkin. That's your name, ain't it? Friends call you Joe?"

"Not if I can help it."

Armstrong laughed. His ears turned red. Then he broke into a fit of coughing and his ears turned scarlet.

"Can I get you some water?" asked Joseph. It wasn't kindness that made him ask. He was fighting back another surge of nausea. This time it was more than the motion of the plane. Armstrong was trying his patience. He found the man obnoxious, if not grotesque. On the other hand, he'd met worse in his line of work. And if it wasn't for the lingering queasiness in his stomach, he probably could have let the man drone on and filtered him out of his consciousness like he filtered out the sound of the engines.

"That's mighty decent of you," said Armstrong, taking out a flask of something or other from the inside pocket of his jacket. He unscrewed the top, took a swig, then turned to Joseph and winked. "I carry my own. Want a drink?" He held out the flask.

Joseph shook his head and watched as Armstrong replaced the cover on the flask, put it back in his jacket and then took a hanky from another pocket which he used to dab the wetness on his lips.

He had salesman's eyes, Joseph thought. Narrow slits that looked at you like you were one of Barnum's suckers.

"Been to Portland before?"

Joseph shook his head.

"Nice town. Friendly. Not as friendly as the south or midwest but friendly enough. Cheaper than Californian cities, of course. That's because of the climate. No one wants to pay to live in rain. Would you?"

He closed his eyes. Maybe if he closed them long enough the guy would go away.

The plane banked suddenly to the left. Joseph felt it in his gut.

"Look down there." Armstrong pointed out the window. "That's the Cascade Range. Willamette National Forest. Greatest batch of lumber left in the United States, not counting

Alaska, of course. Cuttin' it down so fast they can't find enough trucks to haul it to the ports . . ."

. "I thought you said it was National Forest land." Joseph gazed down at the vast carpet of green that reached out to the horizon, broken only by patches of mist that wove through it like a lacy quilt.

"That don't stop the lumber companies. The government is selling it off as fast as the lumbermen can cut it. Mostly to the Japanese. They love American wood."

The plane suddenly banked again, going into a steep descent.

"Looky there! See them mountains to the east?"

Joseph looked where Armstrong pointed. The green had stopped. The mountains below were bare with deep gullies carved into the sides. Through the patches of mist he could see only ghostly stumps.

"Clear cut. Used to be a forest there. Deer, bear, otter, owl. Nothin' lives there now. The rain comes and washes the soil down. Floods the valley. Silt fills up the streams. All to build more houses in Japan." He looked at Joseph with different eyes than before. "Don't make no sense. No sense at all."

"You're a salesman," said Joseph. "It should make sense to you."

Armstrong still had his head turned toward the window. "I said I'm in insurance. Sometimes I do freelance work. Keepin' people honest is my métier, not sellin' them a load of bull. I'm also a father. Two grown kids. The girl's pregnant. I'll be a grandad soon. Wanna leave something for the tyke, you know what I mean?" He turned back toward Joseph and shook his head. "Rate they're going, nothin's gonna be left. Within ten years all the forest'll be gone. Just stumps. You a fisherman?"

"Me?" Joseph blinked his eyes. "No. I'm a city boy. Had a pet guppy once. Had to fish him out of the bowl when a friend of mine fed him a jar of peanut butter for lunch. That's about as close as I got . . ."

"If you were a fisherman you'd know what I mean. Can't eat even the ones you catch. They all got cancers in their bellies from the herbicides and the leaching of heavy metals from the earth."

Joseph thought of the codfish Polly had made the other night and felt something in his stomach start oozing up. It hurt so much he couldn't get his seat belt buckled as the plane headed for the runway and the warning sign flashed on.

It was dark outside. It was raining and he was wet. He cursed himself for having forgotten to bring his mackintosh.

At least the cab was warm, he thought, as it raced down the deserted streets like a bat out of hell—if hell had bats. And if it did have bats, what the hell would they be doing out on a night like this, he wondered?

"What hotel did you say again?" asked the cabby.

"Someplace central," he said.

"Then you got a choice of about a hundred and seventy-six, pal."

"Cheap and clean."

"Contradiction, mate."

"Clean and not too expensive."

"About a dozen. Take your pick."

"Close to a café that serves a decent cup of coffee."

"How about the Metropole."

"Sounds too pretentious."

"Cambridge Arms?"

"Where's that?"

"Near the museum. Small place. Nothing fancy, but they put clean sheets on the bed."

It was a quarter to midnight when he paid the cabby off and went inside to register. The bellboy looked about as tired as he felt.

"Give me the key," Joseph told him, "I'll find my own way up. Here's a buck. Maybe you can get me the evening paper."

He found his room on the second floor. It was just large enough for a double bed and a writing table. There was a closet toilet—the bath was down the hall. But there was a dial phone—the only thing, besides the newspaper, he had ordered.

He had opened his valise and had gotten out his pajamas when he heard the knock at his door.

"Yeah?" he called out.

"Your paper sir," said the voice.

21

"Just slide it underneath."

He took off his clothes and put his nightstuff on. It was his habit to read the paper just before he went to sleep. Polly could never understand it.

"Doesn't it give you bad dreams?" she had asked.

"Just the opposite," he had told her. "It's always filled with stories my nightmares could never top."

He usually took about ten minutes glancing through the pages. However, this evening it only took the headline before he stopped. He read it once and then again. Then he put the paper down.

He lay his head on the pillow and closed his eyes. He tried to fall asleep but the headline kept flashing through his mind like a neon sign: "Prof Against New Pulp Mill Found Dead!"

Chapter 3

In the morning, when he woke up, he placed a call to Saunders.

"Problems," he said.

"Problems are what life's about, Radkin. You were retained to write them up, not bother me with a phone call at 8.00 a.m. . . ."

"Your friend, the professor . . ."

"What about him?"

"He's dead."

There was a moment of silence. Radkin fancied he could hear the gurgling of waters in the background. Somewhere in his olfactory memory he could smell the scent of perfumed steam. "I was afraid of that," Saunders said. "What happened?"

"According to the paper, he was found in his bed late yesterday morning. He didn't wake up."

Silence, again, on the other end of the line.

Joseph felt the heat rising in the back of his neck. "Say, what's going on, Mr Saunders? What's this about?"

"I told you, Radkin. Bright had phoned me several days ago. He was concerned—there were some threatening phone calls . . ."

"I'm not a cop, Mr Saunders. I'm a journalist. I'm not in the protection game. If you thought Bright was in danger and you couldn't get the police to do anything about it, maybe you should have hired a private eye to look after him."

"I did. But it seems I hired him too late. Anyway, it doesn't change the terms of our arrangement. I still want the story on the paper mill. And find out what you can about Bright's death."

"I have the feeling there's something you're not telling me, Mr Saunders." Joseph felt the moisture of his palms dripping down the curved surface of the receiver. There was nothing he hated more than the thought he was being manipulated. Especially when he had no idea what he was being manipulated for.

"Your assignment is to do the story. Whatever you need to know, you'll have to find out for yourself. Where are you calling from?"

He gave him the name and phone number of the hotel. And then he hung up.

Part of him wanted to take the next flight home. The other part wanted the three thousand bucks. And then there was the third part, the shadowy part, the sucker part that wanted to find out what the hell was up.

It was when he opened his luggage to get a change of clothes that he saw it. Sticking out of a compartment on the side. He pulled it out and then tossed it on the bed. It was one of Armstrong's stupid cuff-links with the all-weather ducks. He wondered how it had gotten into his luggage. Perhaps when Armstrong had rummaged through the overhead compartment while the plane was bouncing in the sky. It was curious. But just another curious day in a curious life.

He spent the morning in the library looking things up. McCullough Paper Company was a thriving concern, at least lately, having survived the recession of the early Eighties intact. It had started a couple of generations back as a family operation under the watchful eye of the patriarch, Calvin McCullough. The business had gone public in the Sixties, but even then the family maintained control. The current operations chief was James McCullough, fifty-five years old, who was also the chairman of the board. The corporation had several associated industries: McCullough lumber, based in a place called Happy Valley; a plywood factory located in Coos Bay; and a shipping firm.

From what he could make out, the corporation was modeled on the old school of employer paternalism. They had managed to keep the unions at arm's length by maintaining standards of

24

decent wages, profit-sharing, and a gamut of employee benefits. Of course, the whole thing started to unravel when the recession hit and they were forced to make drastic reductions in the labor force. On the other hand, now that times were good again, McCullough seemed to be better than most at sharing the gold that came pouring in.

The articles in the local press on the fight around the new pulp mill were by-lined Stanley Nickels. Nickels was one of the names Saunders had given him to contact. Joseph gave him a call at the paper and arranged to meet him at a Mexican café near the library for lunch.

Joseph was on the second floor eating a taco when Nickels came in. He recognized him by his hat.

"It's what used to be called a porkpie," Nickels had said on the phone. "Anyway, I'm pretty tall. The tables are on the second floor. Sit by the window if you can. Anything distinctive about you?"

"I don't whistle in the bath," said Joseph. "And—oh, yeah— I still read Pogo."

"You mean Pogo-the-porcupine?"

"Is that what he was? I always thought he was a hedgehog. Anyway someone gave me a book called *The Philosophy of Pogo* back in 1966. I'm still trying to figure it out. From what I can get, he's sort of the Nietzsche of wildlife bohemia."

Joseph held up the book as the tall man in the porkpie hat came in. Calling himself "pretty tall" was like a sumo wrestler calling himself "pretty fat". The guy was at least six foot ten.

"I thought the book was a joke," said Nickels, sitting down with his beef taco.

"That makes two of us. How do you know Saunders?" asked Joseph.

"I don't. My publisher does. But I recognized your name," he said. "Read some of your stuff on the Valdez oil spill that was picked up by the wire service. Not too many people wrote about it from the point of view of the Eskimo."

"It's more fashionable these days to write stories from the point of view of fish," said Joseph.

"That's because most people eat fish rather than Eskimos."

Nickels pointed to the hot sauce. "Try some of that on your burrito. It's really good."

Joseph took a spoonful of the sauce and dumped it in his plate. "What kind of dope do you have on the permit fight around the new pulp mill?" he asked.

"I got a packet of stuff I made up for you," said Nickels, handing him a folder. "Things I pulled from the morgue on McCullough Paper. Anything else you want to know?"

"Maybe you can begin by telling me something about pulp mills," said Joseph. He took a bite of the hot sauce-splashed burrito and thought it would mask the taste of anything—fish or Eskimo.

Nickels raised his eyebrows. "You really are starting at the basics, aren't you?" He rubbed some taco stuffing off his chin. "Well, I guess the first thing of importance you should know is that a new pulp mill costs about five hundred million dollars to build . . ."

"Did you say five hundred thousand or five hundred million?" asked Joseph.

"Five hundred million."

"Who has five hundred million bucks?"

"Banks. Insurance companies . . ."

"And several small African nations—if they combined their assets . . ."

"Modern paper mills are expensive."

Joseph rubbed his nose. The hot sauce had worked its way up to his nasal passages. "I guess." He looked at Nickels, trying to glean a trace of sarcasm in his face. There wasn't—at least as far as he could tell.

"Anyway," Nickels went on, "the next thing you should know is that paper has become a world industry. No such thing as a local market anymore. You're not competing with the mill across the street, but the one across the ocean."

"What does that mean, exactly?"

"It means you better be looking over your shoulder if you don't want to be bought up. We're talking high risk, high stake poker, Radkin."

Joseph picked up his napkin. "All for this?"

"And for your morning paper, your coffee filter, your baby's diaper, your Pogo book . . ."

He held up his hand. "OK. I get your gist . . ."

"We're also talking high tech. You ever see a paper machine?"

"Not lately," said Joseph. "One of my kids tried to dress up like one on Halloween, I think . . ."

"Imagine a football field," Nickels went on without skipping a beat. "Imagine rows of metal rollers, the size of a building, each about a thousand tons, piled three or four on top of one another and spread out along a hundred yards."

"I wouldn't want to be ground up in it, if that's what you're getting at . . ."

"If the state of the art computers that run the thing determined you were wood, you'd probably end up being a newspaper instead of writing for one."

"Right. Now we've established that," said Joseph, "I guess we should add I wouldn't want to drink the waters that come out of its waste pipes."

"Not if it's a bleaching mill—the kind that makes paper white."

"And I suppose McCullough's new pulp mill is a bleaching plant."

"Right," said Nickels. "But there's a twist."

"A twist?"

Nickels finally smiled. "They claim their new mill will turn paper white without dumping dioxin."

"Is that possible?"

"Paper mills use chlorine as their bleaching agent. Chlorine reacts with the pulp, forming effluents of chlorohydrates. There's a couple hundred different chlorohydrates, one of which is dioxin. You can get rid of dioxin two ways. One is by filtering it out—which is almost impossible since we're talking about incredibly minute quantities. The other is by not using a bleaching agent."

"That sounds simple enough," said Joseph.

"If it was simple, it probably would have been done long before now," Nickels replied. "Anyway, DEQ—that's the Department of Environmental Quality—wants proof the new mill won't be dumping more dioxin into the river. So McCullough has invested several million into building a prototype of their new system. DEQ took some samples of their waste water to run a test."

"And?"

"That's the question, isn't it? The permit hearing is the day after tomorrow. DEQ's supposed to present its report then."

"No leaks?"

"Just a trickle. The word is they're clean."

"That's a step forward, isn't it?" said Joseph.

"I'll believe it when I see it," Nickels replied.

"What do you know about a guy named Bright. He's a prof at Meade College—or he was till last night . . ."

"Nathaniel Bright's been a thorn in McCullough's side for a long time."

"Not any more."

"I don't know about that. He might be more danger to them dead than alive. You know what I mean?"

"Not really."

"Bright was pretty well marginalized. He was known as a no-growther, someone who'd be against the mill no matter what. A lot of people here have suffered through some pretty bad times. In the early Eighties half this town was unemployed. They don't want a repeat of that. Besides, there seemed to be something personal between him and old man McCullough."

"Even so . . ."

Nickels cut him off. "And there was something else. You heard of that lumberjack who was killed when he sawed into the tree that was spiked?"

"Yeah," Joseph nodded.

"Some people think Bright was responsible."

"A college prof? They must be a different breed here in Oregon . . ."

"I don't mean he did it himself. But some people say he encouraged whoever did do it by his words. Bright was very angry about what was happening to the forests. And he was very articulate in his opposition."

"That's no reason to think he spiked that tree," said Joseph.

"All I know is that tempers were hot. Still are." Nickels replied.

"But what do you think happened to Bright?"

Nickels pushed back his porkpie hat and looked squarely into Joseph's eyes. "If you want to know that, you're probably going to have to find out for yourself."

"Not much coming down the pipeline, huh?"

Nickels shook his head. "It'll be a while before we can even get a hold of the police report, I bet. Public affairs is trying to play this one way down. Hoping things will cool off. But they won't—unfortunately."

"They won't?"

He looked Joseph straight in the eye again. "No way. They're only going to get hotter!"

Chapter 4

The cab ride across town to Meade College took less than twenty minutes. The campus was situated on the other side of the river and a little to the south, tucked away in a grove of trees and nestled by a brook. With ivy-covered buildings and a peaceful green, it had a languid, near bucolic feel. Inside, however, as he walked into the Admin building, he was struck by the odor of smelly socks.

The provost's office was in a state of disarray. A few fresh-faced students were seated on the floor eating plates of tofu and brown rice emptied from a pot which had been simmering on a camping stove just a moment before.

"They're having a sit-in," the secretary explained as she ushered Joseph through to the inner office. "They're upset that an oak tree is being cut down to make room for the library extension. The problem is that the library's too small and there's nowhere else the extension can go."

"How about building a library in the tree?" suggested Joseph.

"A tree-house library?" The secretary smiled. "Mention that to the provost, why don't you?"

The provost was a slim man with a neatly trimmed beard. If his ears were vegetables, they definitely would have been cabbages. He got up from his desk as Joseph was escorted in and stuck his hand out.

"Hello." He looked down at a note lying on his desk. "Mr Raskin?"

"Radkin." Joseph corrected, reaching across the desk and shaking hands.

"Radkin—ah, yes." He motioned for Joseph to take a seat.

"You wanted to talk about poor Dr Bright." He shook his head and his ears seemed to droop a little. "Such a tragedy! So sudden! I still expect to see him come walking through that door," he said, pointing to the entrance of his office. "I'm afraid his death hasn't quite sunk in."

"I'd come up from San Francisco to interview him about the new pulp paper mill. I understand he was the major force behind the opposition to it," Joseph explained.

The provost folded his hands and set them out in front of him. It would have given him a priestly air, if it hadn't been for the cabbages. "Dr Bright was a very committed man. I've always encouraged our staff to take an active role in the affairs of the broader community . . ."

"By the broader community you mean the city, I take it."

"I mean the community outside our own little academic nest."

"Why did Dr Bright take such an interest in the new paper mill?"

"It's an important issue," said the provost. "What with the plight of our rivers and all. However, it's also an issue that tends to be quite emotive. Dr Bright was an intelligent and well educated man. But sometimes he did tend to forget himself . . ."

"Forget himself?"

"Forget that as an academic his obligation was to rational discourse and not unreasoned rhetoric."

"Maybe he thought it wasn't rational to have so much dioxin in our streams," said Joseph.

"That may be true," replied the provost. "But whether pulp mills account for most of the dioxin is not an established fact. And I suspect most industry pollutes. From what I understand, McCullough Paper Company was better than most at controlling their wastes."

Joseph wrote something in his notebook and then looked up at the provost again. "The article in today's newspaper indicated that Dr Bright lived on campus. Whereabouts?"

Unfolding his hands and getting up from his chair, the provost walked over to the window behind his desk and looked out at the evergreen trees.

"See that cottage?" he said, pointing to a small rustic building by the edge of a little stream. "He moved there about five years ago—right after his wife died."

"Who found him?" asked Joseph.

The provost turned around. "Miss Parker. The woman who takes care of the faculty residences. She was coming in to clean . . ."

"She has the key?"

"Of course."

"And no one heard?"

"As you can see, the cottage is set back . . ."

"I'd like to talk with her," said Joseph.

"Who?"

"Miss Parker. The woman you said found the body."

His face wore a forced smile. "I'm afraid that's impossible. At least right at the moment. She's on holiday, you see . . ."

That's convenient, Joseph thought. "Could I see the cottage?" he asked.

The provost shook his head. "Sorry. The police have cordoned it off till they can determine the actual cause of death." He looked at Joseph, curiously. "What is it you're after?"

"I'd like to find out where Dr Bright was coming from. How did he get such a passionate interest in the paper mill? I mean the air's polluted with smog. He could have been trying to ban the smoke from diesel buses. I read that there's an aluminum plant not so many miles from here that has a slag heap leaching into the Columbia. Some people think there's a connection with the increase in Alzheimer's disease. And just down the road you've got the Trojan Nuclear plant. There's been numerous reports that the nice folk there occasionally let off a bit of radioactive waste. Dr Bright could just as easily have been concerned about them."

"We all choose our battles, I suppose, Mr Radkin."

"Yes. But we all have a reason for the battles that we choose. I'm interested in Dr Bright's."

"I wish I could help you," said the provost, shrugging his shoulders. "Perhaps it was his interest in paper. He was fascinated with its history, you know. In fact, he once gave a seminar. I would have liked to have attended it myself." He let out a little sigh.

"Was there anything troubling him lately?" asked Joseph. "Any problems?"

"Nothing he told me about," said the provost glancing at his watch.

"Sorry to be taking up so much of your time . . ." Joseph said, with a trace of sarcasm in his voice.

"It's just that I have a meeting to attend . . ." the provost said, apologetically. Then he gave Joseph a wicked, little grin. "Would you mind staying here a moment when I leave?"

"Excuse me?" Joseph wondered if he had heard correctly.

The provost pointed toward the window. "I find it easier to go and come through there at the present time. Avoids confrontation, you see. As long as you stay, they'll think I'm in here too. You don't mind, do you?"

"It depends on how long we're talking about," said Joseph. "Ten minutes? An hour? A week?"

"Just give it a minute or two after I leave," said the provost, opening up the window and climbing out. After his feet reached the ground, he turned back to Joseph and said, "Thanks, awfully." Then he scurried off.

Joseph spent a moment perusing the provost's desk. Finding nothing of interest, he left.

"Is he still in there?" a thin young man whose long hair was braided in a pigtail asked as Joseph made his way out.

"No. He left through the window. Said he didn't want a confrontation with you guys yet," Joseph replied.

"He always does that," a tiny blonde girl said. "He thinks we don't know."

"Maybe he's just enjoying himself," Joseph said as he made his way into the hall. "People have very eccentric pleasures when they grow old."

The tiny blonde girl followed him out. "Hey, mister!" she called.

Joseph turned around. "Look," he said. "Let's get one thing straight. In my priorities of life, library extensions come before oak trees. If one of them has to go, I'll choose the oak. Sorry, but that's the way it is. So, no, I don't want to sign your petition."

"We could have both the extension and the oak tree if they weren't so stubborn about the architectural design—but I wasn't going to ask you to sign a petition," she said, coming up to him.

"What then?" He looked at her. Cute face, pixie hair, no shoes, no socks.

"I heard you talking to the secretary about Dr Bright . . ."

She stared at him intently.

"Well?"

"Are you a cop?"

"No. Are you?"

"Me?" For a brief moment her face lit up with a smile. Then she got serious again. "Why are you asking about him then?"

"I'm a journalist. That's my job—to ask questions about people. Even if they're dead. In fact, especially if they're dead."

Her eyes started watering up. She stared at him, silently, as the tears began running down her face.

He took out a hanky from his pocket and handed it to her. "Dry your eyes," he said in a gentler tone of voice. "Is there anyplace around here where we can talk?"

He wondered why it was that all student cafés had sticky tables. It was more than being sloppy drinkers, he thought. It must be that they dusted sugar on everything they bought.

"What's your name?" he asked the blonde girl sitting next to him.

She looked down at her cup of camomile tea as she opened up a packet of honey and stirred it in.

"Ginger," she said.

"I thought all Gingers were red heads."

She shrugged.

"Was Dr Bright one of your teachers?"

"I had him for a seminar once."

"Ecology?"

"History of commodities."

"Commodities?"

34

"Yes. Everyday things like coffee, sugar, salt. He was especially interested in paper. Said it was the barometer of civilization. He thought you could plot the advancement of arts and sciences by the development of paper technology . . ."

"So he wasn't opposed to technology," said Joseph taking a sip of coffee and wishing he hadn't.

She looked at him with surprise. "He didn't want to live in a cave," she said.

"Some people do," he replied.

"He didn't. But he did believe that unrestricted technology was insane."

"So where did he think we were on civilization's plotting chart right now?" Joseph asked.

"About to fall off. We're beyond the point of using resources, Mr Radkin. Now we abuse them. The world produces more than enough paper. We grind up more than enough trees. It's all part of a throw-away mentality. Throw-away wrapping for throw-away lives. Why can't we bring our own bags when we go shopping? In Europe they do. Why can't we brew coffee with reusable filters? And, if we have to use paper, why not keep it its natural color instead of bleaching it white?"

"I thought white was the color of purity," said Joseph.

"And the by-product of purity is dioxin. It's the world's most powerful carcinogen, you know . . ."

"I didn't." He could see she was really getting heated up. "Would you describe Dr Bright as an angry man?" he asked.

"Angry?" She looked at him through eyes of watery blue. "I'd describe him as more concerned than angry. He was a very gentle man."

"Loved by most of his students?"

"Admired," she said.

He looked at her closely. "Admired by some more than others?"

"I suppose so . . . yes."

"Anyone in particular?"

Tears began trickling down her cheeks again. "My friend . . . Katherine . . ."

"She had a crush on him?"

"She liked him very much, yes. They saw a lot of one another."

He nodded in an understanding way and took out his notebook. "What's Katherine's last name, Ginger?"

She glanced at his notebook and then back up at him. There was a frightened look in her eyes. "Why are you writing her name down?" she asked.

"I told you, I'm a journalist. I'd like to talk with her."

Ginger buried her face in her hands and shook her head.

"Look," said Joseph, "I don't write for a scandal sheet. All I'm interested in is finding out what happened to Dr Bright. Maybe your friend Katherine could help."

"But that's just it! Don't you see? She's disappeared!"

"What do you mean, disappeared?"

She shook her head and tears trickled down her cheeks again.

"Ginger, people leave for lots of reasons. Maybe she's upset. Maybe she went home for a while. Did you contact her parents?"

She shook her head again.

He smiled. "Well, that's it then. She went home for a little comforting. That's normal, isn't it?"

"You don't understand!" she cried. "She hated her parents! She'd never go there!"

"Calm down," he said, handing her back his hanky. "When was the last time you saw her?"

"Several days ago," she said, wiping her eyes. "It was really weird. I was coming over to her place to meet her . . ."

"She wasn't home?"

"No. I saw her as I came by. She was getting into a fancy car. She was with a man. A really gross-looking guy. Looked like he had burns over half his face. And when he noticed me I could feel the temperature drop about ten degrees . . ."

"So she was with a weird guy. So what? People have strange tastes, Ginger. Especially when they're in college. They like to try new things. Like going out with gross-looking men . . ."

"But it wasn't only that. She looked weird, herself."

"How so?"

"Her eyes. She looked almost hypnotized."

"Maybe she was on something."

Ginger shook her head. "Katherine was pretty clean. Maybe an occasional hit of pot now and then but nothing more than that."

"Are you sure?"

"I know her pretty well. I'm really concerned about her, Mr Radkin," she said, handing the wet handkerchief back.

"I'll see what I can find out," he said. "Give me her name and address."

"McCullough. Katherine McCullough. She lives in that funky building on the corner of Woodland Street."

He stared at her. "She wouldn't be related to the McCulloughs of paper fame, would she?"

Ginger nodded. "James McCullough—the guy who runs it—that's her old man."

Chapter 5

The address Ginger had given him was a ramshackle cottage near campus. An archway cut into a wild hedge provided an opening for persons under five foot two. Anyone else had to duck their head.

If you were a weed, you could have done worse than to have made the front yard there your home. They grew with abandon—except in a small area that was fenced off. There the corn reached as high as a grasshopper's eye. The lettuce had big chunks bitten out. The cucumbers looked like emaciated string-beans. And the tomatoes weren't worth talking about. It reminded him of his garden back in San Francisco.

"You might try using just a little bit of pesticide," he had once told Polly. "Watered down, of course."

She had looked at him in horror. "In my organic garden?"

He had pointed to a marauding band of snails.

"As long as they're alive, we're alive," she had said.

The wooden porch was missing a few floor boards, he noticed as he made his way, precariously, to the door. He pulled open the screen and confronted the words—"Think Globally, Act Locally"—painted in bright green. He gave a knock.

A man opened the door. He had a narrow face with sunken cheeks, a hawk-like nose and a scraggly beard that looked like it had been borrowed from a Spanish conquistador. In his mind, Joseph compared him, somewhat unfavorably, to one of the scrawny vegetables.

He looked at Joseph suspiciously.

"I'd like to speak with Katherine McCullough. Is she around?" asked Joseph.

The man shook his head.

38

"Can you tell me where I can find her?"

He shook his head again.

"When's she coming back?"

He shrugged.

"You live here?" asked Joseph.

He shook his head and pointed to the garden.

"You're the gardener?"

He nodded.

A man of few words, Joseph thought as he took a card from his wallet and wrote a number on the back. "Here," he said, handing it to him. "Do me a favor and give this to her when she returns. Tell her to give me a call." He gazed into the man's face to see if he was comprehending him. "All right?"

The man was staring at the card. He nodded.

Joseph had reached the archway and was stooping down to leave when he heard a whistle.

He turned around and saw the man trotting over to him. When he got next to Joseph, he took a pencil and a pad of paper from his pocket and scribbled, "You're Radkin?"

Joseph nodded. "I'm a journalist for *Investigations Magazine*." He pointed to the card which the man was holding in his hand. "Pick it up sometimes. They've got a good gardening column . . ." He glanced over at the weeds. "But maybe you wouldn't be interested."

"I've read your stuff," the man wrote on his pad.

"Yeah?" said Joseph, always pleased to meet an admirer.

"Yeah," the guy wrote. "Lot of liberal claptrap. Why do you want to see Katherine?" The man held out his pad and narrowed his eyes.

"I'm doing a story on the opposition to the new pulp mill. I wanted to interview Professor Bright, but it seems he's unavailable. A girl I met at his college told me Bright was one of Katherine's teachers. She also said that Katherine disappeared. You know anything about that?"

The guy scribbled something on his pad again. He didn't answer Joseph's question but wrote instead, "Where you off to?"

"Back to town," Joseph said.

"You have a car?"

Joseph shook his head. "I'll get a cab back at the college."

The guy's fingers moved swiftly as he wrote, "Forget it. I'll give you a lift."

It was a beat-up red Toyota station wagon with a missing fender on the right and a smashed-in door on the left. Joseph had to enter on the driver's side and scoot his body down in order to get to the passenger seat.

The back was all cluttered with junk. Among the trash there was also a mattress and blankets as well as a wooden crate that held an alcohol stove.

And there was something else, too. Joseph didn't see it at first as it was so small. And when he did see it, he thought it was a rat. But it wasn't. It had a nose that looked like a soggy chunk of coal and miniature wolfin paws. Zoologically speaking, it was probably of the canine persuasion.

"Nice car," said Joseph, wondering whether the guy lived in there. He looked back again. "Nice dog?"

The man nodded.

"You know Katherine very well?"

He shook his head. And then he clammed up.

They had been driving for about fifteen minutes down a street that seemed to have no beginning nor an end but just went on and on through similar neighborhoods of monotonous houses that all reminded him of bologna sandwiches on white bread with mayonnaise when suddenly they pulled into a parking lot and stopped.

"You mind telling me where we are?" asked Joseph, as the man opened the door and got out.

The dog jumped out as well. The man motioned for Joseph to come along.

Joseph got out and followed. The man was standing before a door, fiddling with the lock. The mut was yapping at his heels. Then, bending down, the man opened the oversize pocket of his jacket and the mut jumped in.

He wondered why the guy bothered with a lock at all when he pushed open the door, exhibiting the emptiness inside. There were a couple of desks and some boxes filled with papers. On each desk was a battered typewriter. There was also a telephone with a large object covered up beside it. And something else. Over by the far side of the room was a life-size cardboard cut-out of a brawny logger wearing a hard hat and holding out a chainsaw. It was mounted on a base with a spring attachment.

"What's that for?" asked Joseph, pointing at the cardboard contraption.

The man, who had picked up some mail that had been shoved underneath the door, turned around and gave a whistle. At that the dog jumped out of his pocket and, in one enormous leap, sprang at the logger, grabbing the chainsaw in its tiny mouth.

The logger went down to the floor. The dog hopped off and the logger popped back up again.

"Very nice," said Joseph. "That trick must win a lot of friends among the workers."

Taking out his pad, the man wrote, "Strictly self-defense."

"I guess you come in contact with a lot of chainsaw murderers," said Joseph.

The guy sat down in front of a typewriter, rolled in a fresh sheet of paper and whipped out a few lines. Then, unrolling the paper he had typed on, he handed it to Joseph.

Joseph read it aloud. '"I suppose a big-time reporter like yourself wouldn't find this awe-inspiring. But we make do without the aid of multinational corporations."'

He looked at the scrawny man and asked, "We who?"

The man leaned down, opened one of the boxes on the floor and pulled out a tabloid. He handed it to Joseph.

Joseph gave it a once over. "*Midnight Special*", he said. "Nice name."

He glanced through the pages. Half the articles had the same by-line. He looked over at the guy who seemed to be inspecting him closely. "You wouldn't be Wolenski, would you?" he asked.

The man nodded and gave him a look as if to say "How'd you know?"

"Lucky guess," Joseph replied. He pointed to the paper. "How long you been in business?"

Wolenski stuck a finger in the air and crooked it in half.

41

Then he wrote on his pad, "Anytime we can raise the dough. Times are tough . . ."

"You're telling me!" said Joseph. He noticed that the masthead had the same quote as the one he saw on Katherine's front door.

"Ecology's your bag, I gather."

"Ecology is everyone's bag," Wolenski wrote. "The ecosystem is going to hell in a handcar."

Joseph glanced at the headlines screaming out from the front page. "Right-Wing Cult In League With Loggers!"

"Pretty heavy stuff," said Joseph, handing the tabloid back.

"Keep it," Wolenski wrote. "Lots more where that came from."

Folding the tabloid, Joseph put it in his pocket. "Was Katherine working with you on this paper, by any chance?"

He nodded. Then he wrote, "She had some good sources."

"I bet!" said Joseph. "Did her father know what she was up to?"

Wolenski shook his head and scribbled. "She wrote under a different name."

"What?"

"TARA." He wrote each letter in caps.

"When was the last time you talked with her?"

He stuck three fingers in the air.

"Three days ago? Where was she?"

He shrugged.

"You mean you talked to her on the telephone?" Joseph looked at him curiously. "How . . ."

Wolenski went over to the telephone and pulled off a cloth from an object at its side, displaying the terminal of a microcomputer. Sitting down in front of it, he turned it on and typed. "Hello," the computer said in a soft but distinctly masculine voice, "My name is Hal."

Joseph smiled. "Pretty fancy stuff for someone who doesn't have the aid of a multinational corporation."

"I'm a present from Tara."

"And this is how you speak to her over the phone," Joseph mused aloud.

"Yes," said Hal. "I miss her."

"I can imagine," Joseph replied. He thought a moment and then he asked, "What was Katherine's relationship with Bright?"

"He was her teacher," said Hal.

"Anything more?"

Wolenski's fingers hesitated over the keys. "You'd have to ask Katherine," said Hal, finally.

"Was he Tara's teacher as well?"

"Wolenski was Tara's teacher," said Hal.

"I understand Bright's wife died some years ago. He had a daughter, didn't he?"

"Yes," said Hal. "She's a lawyer for the Wilderness Commission."

"I'd like to talk to her." Joseph, looked closely at Wolenski as his fingers darted over the keyboard.

"Be my guest."

"You know where she lives?"

"Someplace in the Portland area. I wouldn't be surprised if she were listed in the telephone directory."

"Well, if we can find it, would you mind dropping me off there?"

Wolenski turned back around and stared at him. Joseph saw the glint in his eye. He took out his pad of paper and wrote, "Sure, man—why not?"

Wolenski let him off on the corner of 23rd and Overton in the Northwest quarter of town. The address was a two-story Victorian a few yards up Overton with a big poster in the window that read "Save Our Fine Old Houses". It was easy to see why. Down the block two fine old houses were boarded up. Next door, a bulldozer was flattening another—at least what remained of it. On the other side was just an empty lot.

He climbed the stairs and stood on the porch a moment with his finger poised over the bell. Inside he could hear voices— one male and one female. The discussion, if one could call it that, was loud, though the specific words were muffled in the background.

Suddenly, the door was pulled abruptly open and a tall,

angular man dressed in a business suit, looking somewhat ruffled, burst out. He seemed startled by Joseph's presence.

"Can I help?" he asked with note of extreme annoyance.

"My name's Joseph Radkin," he said. "Is Abigail Bright in?"

"She's in but she isn't seeing anyone today. Her father just died," the man said curtly.

"I understand," said Joseph. "The thing is I've just come up from San Francisco. A good friend of her father's asked me to stop by."

"I'm not sure you do understand," said the man. "But, then again, neither do I." And with that he turned around and shouted, "Abigail! Someone to see you!" Then he stomped down the stairs, leaving the door slightly ajar.

"Who is it Henry?" called a voice.

"Joseph Radkin. I'm a friend of William Saunders," Joseph called back, pushing the door open a little wider.

"Can't you come back some other time?" asked the voice. It sounded weary.

"It would be difficult. I'm leaving town soon," said Joseph, pushing the door open wider still and sticking his head inside. "I won't keep you more than a moment . . ."

"Oh, very well," said the voice. "Come in."

"Thank you," said Joseph, walking inside. It wasn't what he expected. The place was very sleek and modern with French impressionism on the walls accentuated by track lighting. The furniture was Danish, blond and stylish.

The woman on the white cloth couch was probably in her mid-thirties. Her light-brown hair brushed her shoulders in billows of curls. She was trim and polished. Her face, however, had a tired pallor.

She got up from the couch as he came in. "I don't really remember a William Saunders," she said. "Am I supposed to?"

"Mr Saunders is on the board of the magazine I write for."

"What magazine is that?" she asked, sitting back down and motioning for him to sit in the chair across from her.

"*Investigations*. Do you know it?" he asked, following her instructions.

44

"Yes. You did a story on the migrant labor force recently . . ."

"One of my colleagues," said Joseph.

"It was very good." She stared at him questioningly. "What is it that you wanted?"

"Mr Saunders asked me to offer his condolences." Joseph pursed his lips. Then he said, "I'm sure your father's death must have been a great shock . . ."

"It wasn't unexpected," she replied.

She caught him off-guard and he looked at her with surprise. Even so, he took advantage of the opportunity. "Mr Saunders said your father phoned him a few days ago. He said your father sounded concerned about something . . ."

"He was concerned about many things. What did Mr Saunders mention in particular?"

"It seems your father wasn't clear. Though Mr Saunders assumed it had something to do with the upcoming permit hearing for the new pulp mill. Your father had planned to testify, I believe."

Abigail nodded. "Yes, he did."

"Did he have any special information that he was going to present?"

She looked at him curiously. So he added, "I'm asking this because the early editions of the paper made it seem the cause of his death was somewhat suspect . . ."

"If you mean information that wasn't easily attainable by others, I'd say probably not. My father was an articulate spokesman for environmental reform. He had a certain credibility because of his academic position. Therefore his testimony was important. But not important enough for someone to kill him in order to have it stopped."

"I understand you work for a public interest law firm."

"Yes. Mellon and Browne. You met Mr Mellon, I believe, on his way out."

"Did your firm have anything to do with the hearing for the permit application?"

"Only in a round-about way," she said. "We're representing the Wilderness Commission's suit to prevent the logging of the Bear Creek Forest."

"How does that fit in with McCullough Paper's application to build a pulp mill?" he asked.

"McCullough Lumber is a subsidiary of McCullough Paper. They own the lumber rights to Bear Creek. Clear cutting the forest would give them easy access to cash."

He rubbed the side of his face. "Excuse a stupid question," he said. "But why are you trying to save Bear Creek?"

She stared at him a moment before she spoke. "You're not familiar with the area, I suppose."

He shook his head.

"It's one of the last major stands of old growth forest that remains in Oregon. Have you ever been in an old growth forest, Mr Radkin?"

"No. I'm ashamed to say I haven't."

"It's an experience you should try sometime."

"I'm a city boy," he explained. "For me it would be like a trip to Mars. I must admit I'm more interested in people than trees."

"Without trees there wouldn't be any people," she said. "The forest is our heritage. Once it's lost, it can never be reclaimed."

"Perhaps," said Joseph. "I understand a logger was recently killed by someone who nailed a spike into a tree. Did that have anything to do with Bear Creek?"

"Yes. Before the courts gave us our injunction some people, whose motives I appreciate but whose tactics I strongly disagree with, decided to take matters into their own hands. There was a lack of reason on both sides. Unfortunately things went a little too far . . ."

"Then you got the injunction?"

"The injunction was temporary—for a cooling-down period. We're trying to reach an agreement with McCullough Lumber to cease operations in Bear Creek until we can work out a compromise."

"Was your father involved in this?"

She was silent for a moment. Then she shook her head.

Joseph noticed that her expression was becoming strained. It made him hesitate, but only for a moment.

"Would you mind if I asked a delicate question?"

46

She looked at him with some surprise. "My goodness, haven't you? I suppose you mean more delicate. In which case, it just depends on what you want to know. I must tell you, though, I have a terrible headache and I'm going to have to cut this conversation short very soon . . ."

"Were you close to your father? I mean, were you on good terms?"

"My father was a very special man, Mr Radkin," she said. "He cared for the world—perhaps too much. And perhaps the world didn't care enough about him. But he lived his life the way he wanted to live it. And he made it very clear to me that one should never mourn a life fulfilled."

"But it's possible your father didn't die a natural death," said Joseph.

"What death is natural, Mr Radkin?" Her brown eyes seemed to be sparkling. He noticed they had fiery flakes of red.

The logic of her response had him clearly stymied.

"Did you know my father?" she asked, again focusing her gaze on him.

He shook his head. "No. I never had the privilege . . ."

"Then there are many things you wouldn't understand . . ."

"Yes. I'm sure that's right . . ."

"For instance," she said, "the fact that for the last five years he was slowly dying of cancer."

Chapter 6

He called Nickels from the first payphone that he met:

"Just spoke to Bright's daughter, Abigail . . ."

"What did you find out?"

"Not much. She's a tough cookie. Left me with more questions than answers."

"Yeah, I've seen her in court."

"But I did get the clear impression that she thinks her father committed suicide. Says he was dying of cancer."

"Seems strange the police wouldn't have suggested that. It sure would take them off the hook."

"Or maybe some hotshot reporter jumbled up his report. You want to check it out?"

"Will do. What else she have to say?"

"She told me a little about the Bear Creek mess. What do you know about that?"

"Big cause among the woodland set. Became a flash point in the fight between lumber interests and eco groups—growth and no-growth. It all boiled down to a fucking bird."

"Sorry—I didn't get that."

"A bird—the spotted owl. That's how they got their injunction. Environmentalists claimed if the forest was cut down the species would die out."

"Sounds to me like it was more than that," said Joseph.

"It was. But the loggers saw the symbolism. Their jobs were at stake—or so they thought. And these effete, college kids and middle-class Yuppies wanted to take their livelihood away for the sake of a bird."

"Speaking of birds, what do you know about James McCullough's daughter? Her name's Katherine . . ."

"Nothing—except she exists."

"That's a matter of conjecture. How about a news sheet—The *Midnight Special*?"

"The literary organ for some environmentalist nuts. Why?"

"I have reason to believe she's been writing for them under a pen name—'Tara'."

Nickels let out a chuckle. "Old man McCullough would really love that. You think he knows?"

"My source thinks not."

"Well, I wouldn't like to be the one to tell him."

"I'd like to interview him," said Joseph.

"Good luck!"

"Can you get me his address and home phone number?"

"I can try. Call me back in a half hour."

"Great. Before you hang up, is there a decent bookstore around here? And someplace to get a cup of coffee."

"Where are you?"

"23rd and Overton."

"Go down to Burnside and take a left to 10th. The name is Powell's. Coffee and books. It's a city institution."

He hadn't gone more than a hundred feet before he saw him. He was standing before the open tailgate of the station wagon, warming his hands on a metal cup. Behind him, on the tailgate, was a pot of water boiling on an alcohol stove.

"You've been waiting for me?" asked Joseph walking up to him. He could see the dog peeking from his pocket.

Wolenski took out his pad. "You got money to waste on cabs?" he wrote. He showed it to Joseph who shrugged.

Stuffing his writing pad back in his pocket, Wolenski packed up his stuff and slammed the tailgate shut.

"Powell's," said Joseph, squeezing himself in as Wolenski held the driver's door open. "You know where that is?"

Wolenski nodded. He started up the engine and turned to Joseph with a questioning look.

"You want to know about my conversation with Abby? Is that it?"

He made an expression which seemed to say he wanted something in exchange for services rendered. At the same

49

time, he pulled out abruptly from the parking space, jolted forward about twenty feet and then slammed on his brakes for a light.

"One thing I found out is that she's a little more cautious than guys like you." Joseph reached down and fastened his seat belt.

Wolenski lifted his eyebrows. One side of his mouth went up in a look of sarcasm. The light changed to green and he lurched forward again.

"Well, I suppose she does believe in the art of compromise," Joseph replied. "But from what I hear, the injunction stopped Bear Creek from being cut down. Not the tree spike."

Wolenski looked like he would have let out an ironic laugh if he were able.

"OK—so the injunction's run out. And they're trying to replace it with a promise. But that's better than an axe!"

Wolenski made a honking sound through his nostrils. At the same time he turned sharply left, cutting off a delivery truck.

"If they break their promise, you can always try for an injunction again."

He gave Joseph a nasty look.

"Watch the road," Joseph cautioned. He stared at Wolenski's profile. "Convince me I'm wrong."

Wolenski slammed on his brakes, stopping the station wagon in the middle of the busy street. He took out his pencil, licked the point and began to write on his pad while the cars behind him sounded their horns.

"It takes a couple of weeks to get an injunction," he wrote. "The Oregon courts won't give it to them. They're in the industry's pocket. You have to go to the 5th circuit in San Francisco. It takes about two weeks at the best to get your appeal . . ." He tore off the page he had written on and handed it to Joseph.

"That's pretty fast," said Joseph, reading it. "Most courts work on the time frame of Jupiter."

"That's the best you can expect!" he wrote. "And even then they could clear cut half the forest before you could get a decision!"

He held out the pad to Joseph and glared. Behind them the people kept blaring their horns.

Joseph took the pad from him, turned the page and wrote, "They'd need a lot of lumberjacks to work that fast!"

"Maybe twenty years ago, pal!" wrote Wolenski, grabbing the pad back. "Now they don't even need to use chainsaws!" He tore off the page, handed it to Joseph and continued writing on the next. "They've got these machines—built like metal Godzillas. Enormous cranes with grotesque teeth set inside steel jaws. They can bite through a tree in less than a second." He tore another page, handed it on and continued. "Fifty of those babies could eat up half a forest in one week's time."

"Just for lunch, I bet," said Joseph. "I wonder what they do for dinner?"

Wolenski seemed truly offended by that remark. He used his pencil to make slashing marks on the paper. "YOU WON'T BE LAUGHING WHEN ALL THE FORESTS ARE GONE, MAN!"

"I won't be laughing when the rivers turn to salt or when plutonium dust settles on my milk or when acid rain eats through my roof or when radon turns my brain to mush either. So I'd like to get all my laughing done now. I'm sorry if you mind."

"I DO MIND!" Wolenski shouted on paper. Then he turned around to the cars blaring their horns behind him and made an obscene gesture.

The station wagon lurched forward again for about a hundred yards, turned left in spite of the "No Turn" sign, and then pulled over to the side. Wolenski took his pad and wrote, "I got a word for guys like you . . ."

Joseph grabbed Wolenski's pencil and gave him a mean smile. "Not without this you don't," he said.

Wolenski glared at him with daggers.

"Just take me to Powell's," said Joseph. "Or should I walk?"

His beard seemed to bristle as he pointed to the building that loomed outside Joseph's window. A big sign fixed on it read: "Powell's Books".

It was the biggest bookstore he had ever seen. One of the biggest anyway. It was so big that when he came in they handed him a map.

"Can I help you, sir?" said a young woman with a sincere look in her eyes.

"Possibly," he said. "Could you direct me to the forest?"

"Excuse me?" She looked at him curiously.

"I'm not exactly sure what I want, you see. I have some keywords in mind: forest, trees, ecology, lumber industry, paper, mills, etc."

She smiled, probably thankful that he wasn't just another nut. She circled several areas on a map which she then handed him.

He spent about twenty minutes ambling around, pulling things off the shelf and giving them a look. In the end, he selected four books and was about to take them to the counter when he spied a sign which read, "This way to the café."

He followed the arrow.

It was a large room with many tables, very light, with shelves of magazines and newspapers and piles of books that were studiously being read amidst the fragrant smell of fresh espresso.

He felt the warm glow of an inner smile.

"Is it all right to bring books in here to read?" he asked the woman behind the coffee counter.

"If you're careful," she replied. "And we appreciate it if you bring in no more than four—at a time."

He nodded. "That's all I can read—at a time, anyhow."

"Then enjoy yourself," she said. "What can I get you?"

He ordered a café latte without the sprinkles and took it to a nearby table. He made himself comfortable and then settled down for an extended read—paging through the books.

In the end, he settled on two and, on his way out, reshelved the others.

"Do you have a phone here?" he asked the cashier as he tendered the money.

"By the bathroom," he said, pointing straight back.

He left his package and went to make his call.

"You have no idea how much trouble this was," Nickels said as he gave him the address and the telephone number.

"Trouble is what life's about," said Joseph.

"If that's your philosophy then you're certainly in the right profession," Nickels replied.

After he hung up, he dropped another quarter in the slot and dialled again.

"McCullough residence." It was a woodchopper's voice—tough and throaty.

"I'd like to speak with Mr James McCullough."

"I'll see if he's in. Who's calling?"

"This is Joseph Radkin. Tell him it concerns his daughter."

He waited a minute or so and then another voice came on, deep and brusque. "McCullough, here. Who the hell are you?"

"Joseph Radkin. I'd like to speak to you about your daughter."

"I didn't ask for your name! I asked who the hell you are!"

"You mean my profession or my bank balance?"

"Listen, if you think you can blackmail . . ."

"Whoa—we're not talking kidnapping here, are we?"

"Who are you? What the hell do you want?"

"Joseph Radkin. I'm a journalist. I'd like to talk to you about your daughter."

The voice seemed to soften a bit. "What did you want to say?"

"I have some information about her that might interest you."

"Go on . . ."

"Not over the phone," said Joseph. "I'd like to come to your house . . ."

The voice was quiet on the other end.

"Mr McCullough? Are you still there?"

"Yes. I'm very busy tonight . . ."

"Too busy to talk about your daughter? It won't take long."

McCullough hesitated a moment. His voice had a trace of fatigue or, maybe, resignation. "I've got an important meeting in an hour."

"I'll come now," Joseph replied.

53

Chapter 7

He saw him out of the corner of his eye—warming his hands on the metal cup, tailgate down, water on the boil—still at the same spot he had left him almost an hour before.

Joseph walked up to the scrawny man in front of the beat-up Toyota.

Wolenski glared and handed him a note: "What took you so long?" it read. Then, quickly dousing the alcohol flame and closing up the tailgate, he loped over to the driver's door and pulled it open.

"Don't you have something better to do with your life?" asked Joseph, sliding himself across the seat to the passenger side of the car.

Wolenski climbed inside and shut the door after him. "Figure maybe I can learn something from a big shot like you," he wrote on his pad. Then he looked at Joseph, almost smiled, and silently mouthed the words, "Where to, man?"

Joseph took out his notebook and opened it up. "Dunthorp. You know where that is?"

Wolenski nodded and started up the Toyota.

"How far is it?"

He made the sign for twenty by flashing the fingers of his hand four times as he pulled out from the curb.

"Keep your eyes on the road!" Joseph shouted, cringing as a bread van squealed to a halt, avoiding them by inches. He glared at his driver. "Where'd you get your license? Poland?"

Wolenski headed down to the river front and took the first freeway entrance to the south. Once he was on the highway, he pressed the pedal to the metal, letting the engine run as fast as she could go—which was about as speedy as a lame dog chasing a slug across a muddy road.

There wasn't any sign on the highway for Dunthorp. Either you knew where it was and had business there or you weren't invited to get off.

The wooded hills were peaceful above the highway that followed the meandering flow of the Willamette River. The trees stood tall in twenty-acre parcels of land. The houses that were set back a good distance from the road had a marvelous time pretending they were in the wilderness. Of course, in a car it only took three minutes from house to wilderness and down to the highway again. But that was very convenient for the executives who needed to be at their offices every morning by at least half past ten.

The concrete wall surrounding the McCullough mansion had an iron gate-house entrance. Wolenski got out of the station wagon and stretched as Joseph made his exit.

Mounted on one of the pillars of the gate-house was a squawk box. Joseph pushed the button. A few minutes later, he pushed it again.

Through the static, a voice could be heard saying, "Who is it?"

"Joseph Radkin to see Mr McCullough," he answered back.

The gate was buzzed open and Joseph walked through, closing it behind. Before him lay a labyrinthine path.

McCullough was what the magazines often called "distinguished". Certainly his tall stature, his chiseled jaw and his greying temples did nothing to diminish that description.

He met Joseph at the door. Looked him up and down. Didn't seem to particularly like what he saw but let him in anyway.

"You've got about five minutes of my time," he said, leading Joseph into a study that adjoined the central hall. On the floor was strewn a bear-skin rug. On top of that was a sleeping dog—Joseph didn't know its make—who looked like he might have caught the bear in his teeth. The dog was sleeping before a stone fireplace which was guarded by a stag—its head, at least.

McCullough lit up a cigar which he had taken from his desk. He turned to Joseph, puffing smoke. He glared and said nothing more than, "Speak!"

"Nice place you've got," said Joseph, admiringly.

"Get to the point!" McCullough glanced at his watch. "You've got four minutes."

"That's a hell of an attitude for someone's who's missing a daughter!" Joseph said, staring back into powerful grey eyes that seemed as cold as the glass ones in the stag.

The words seemed to make McCullough's face slack, but not much. "What do you know about her?" he asked.

"Look," said Joseph, "if you want to talk, let's. But not like this. I came here to have a reasonable discussion. I don't want anything from you except a little information. In return, there might be some I can give."

McCullough chewed down on his cigar, but the bristles on his back relaxed. He pointed to a chair. "Sit down," he offered, as he himself leaned against the desk. "Maybe I've been a little—abrupt. As I told you, this evening's a bad time for me to have guests. My daughter's been gone from this house for several years now. If what you have to say is so urgent, I'm not sure why you couldn't give it to me over the phone . . ."

"I suppose I felt I needed to talk with you in person," said Joseph, "because of the delicacy of the issue."

"What issue are we talking about?" asked McCullough.

"The death of Dr Nathaniel Bright."

The spoken name made McCullough's face tense up again. "Are you implying that my daughter had something to do with that?"

Joseph shrugged. "She was one of the last people to see him before he died." Whether or not this was true, it had its intended reaction.

"Who hired you?" asked McCullough, giving Joseph a searching look, as if there was something he had missed the first time.

"I'm a journalist. Not a private investigator," he said. "I was doing a story on your new pulp paper mill. My publisher wanted me to look into Bright's death. I went to interview the provost at his college. That's how I found out about Bright and your daughter."

"From the provost?" asked McCullough.

"No. One of the students overheard me questioning his secretary. She followed me out and told me about Katherine."

McCullough had gone over to the fireplace. He took a poker from the side and used it to scrape the remnants of a former fire. "What did she tell you?"

"Just that Katherine had been seeing a great deal of Professor Bright and that she had gone missing around the time of his death."

He seemed to be musing something over in his mind as he poked through yesterday's embers. "How much do you want?" he asked.

"For what?" Joseph replied, trying to gauge what was going through McCullough's mind at that moment.

"To keep my daughter out of it . . . your story that is."

He looked over at the man who no longer seemed so dignified. "Mr McCullough, I don't write for the tabloids. I have no interest in your daughter except in so far as she can help me understand what happened to Bright. And I have no interest in him except in so far as he can help me understand the fuss around your paper plant. However, what I can't understand is why you seem so unconcerned about your daughter's whereabouts."

He turned back around. The poker was still in his hands and he was gripping it so hard his knuckles were turning white.

"Does it seem that I'm unconcerned about my daughter? Well, let me tell you a few things. She left this house over two years ago—as soon as she received rights to her grandfather's trust fund. She went to Meade College. That was her choice, not mine. She fell in with a bad group there. And she disowned us. You say she disappeared last week. As far as we're concerned, she disappeared a long time before."

"But she's still your daughter," said Joseph. "Despite all that. I'm sure you'd want to know . . ."

"She's done great damage to this family, Mr . . ."

"Radkin. Joseph Radkin."

"Mr Radkin. She's done things we can never forgive."

"She must have done some terrible things then," said Joseph.

"Not in a legal sense, in case I've juiced your journalistic appetites. It's more a matter of broken trusts."

"On which end?"

"Families are the basic units in our society, Mr Radkin. Strong families survive. Weak ones perish. Look back in history. Families are the atoms which build social cohesion. Weak societies are built of weak units. Strong societies have . . ."

"Patriarchs," Joseph put in.

"That word might be out of fashion now. But it's true, nonetheless. Always has been. Always will be."

"May I ask you a question?" said Joseph, trying to shift gears fast.

"As a man, yes. As a journalist, no. I don't give interviews to the press. I have a legal team with strict instructions to deal with anyone who invades my privacy in print."

"I have no intention of invading your privacy," said Joseph. "Unless your privacy comes before the public trust."

"My business is another matter entirely. If our new pulp mill interests you, I'd be more than happy to arrange for you to meet with our public information officer. All your questions will be patiently answered by people far more knowledgeable . . ."

He was interrupted by a knocking at the door. A balding man with metal spectacles pushed half-way down his nose stuck his head in without waiting for a response.

"Jim," he said, "we need you upstairs. We've got Thompson of First National on the horn . . ."

McCullough made a sign and suddenly the man stopped. "This is Mr Radkin. He's a journalist who was kind enough to stop by with some information about my daughter . . ."

The bald head looked at Joseph and a stubby finger pushed at the spectacle frames. Then, glancing back at McCullough, he said, "He's on the phone now, Jim. We've got to make a decision."

"I'm coming," said McCullough. Then, turning to Joseph he said, "Sorry to cut you off, Mr Radkin. Give me your number and I'll have one of my people contact you."

"Thanks," said Joseph, realizing there was no point in

arguing. Sometimes you win. Sometimes you lose. This time he lost. He took out a card and wrote his number on the back. "I'm staying at the Cambridge Arms."

"Never heard of it, but I'm sure it's a fine place," said McCullough, putting the card in his pocket. "Haveck will show you out."

As McCullough and the bald-headed man left the room, a stocky ex-boxer type dressed in a butler suit came in. One side of his face was severely scarred, as if he had been half-roasted in a fire—coming in or going out. He had gentle eyes for someone so tough, thought Joseph as the man held the door open for him.

He was leaving the study when he saw her coming down the stairs. She was very blonde and slim and what clothes covered her sleek body were probably the best. She glanced at him as if he wasn't there and then grabbing a fur which was slung over the bottom railing of the stairs, without a word, dashed out, slamming the door behind.

All she left was a little cloud of French perfume for him to remember her by.

"Who was that?" asked Joseph as Haveck opened the door for him.

"The boss' daughter," Haveck replied. He said it without a hell of a lot of respect. And Joseph thought his eyes didn't look so gentle anymore.

Chapter 8

The red Jaguar convertible with the license plate that shouted, DO IT! was racing down the drive, splattering pebbles and dust. Even though the top was down, Joseph could only see her blonde hair trailing out.

The iron gate clicked shut behind him with a metallic sound which echoed through the stillness of the adjoining woods. Beyond, the fading sun was sending shadows through the trees. Parked off the drive, in a little cove, Wolenski's car seemed empty.

Joseph walked up to the station wagon and poked his head inside the open window. The car had a faint mildew odor mixed with one of rust. He pulled his head back out and looked around. Wolenski was nowhere to be seen.

Then he felt a pebble hit him on the back of the head.

Looking in the direction it was thrown, Joseph saw Wolenski half hidden in the brush motioning to him.

"What's going on?" asked Joseph, walking over to Wolenski's hiding spot.

Wolenski put his finger to his lips and then grabbing Joseph by his arm, pulled him into the bracken.

Just as Joseph was about to launch a strong protest, Wolenski pointed back toward the road. A black Chrysler appeared. It slowed down as it approached Wolenski's station wagon and then stopped.

Two men in suits got out and were nosing around the Toyota. One of them, who looked like he had an injured arm, had lowered the tailgate and was starting to rummage through the boxes.

"What do you have in those boxes?" Joseph asked Wolenski, feeling his patience run thin.

Wolenski put his finger to his lips again as a warning. He had a worried look.

"What do you mean, keep my voice down!" Joseph felt his temper rise. "I'm here on business! I was invited, for Christ's sake!"

Joseph pulled himself away from Wolenski's grip and was stomping through the underbrush.

"Hey, you!" he shouted to the man who was standing outside the station wagon. "What do you want?"

The man outside the station wagon was short and ugly with a face like a pit bull terrier.

"This car belong to you, bud?"

"No," said Joseph. "It belongs to the idiot who gave me a ride . . ."

He started saying that when he had reached the roadway. He never got the whole thing out. The short guy had grabbed him by the collar with a grip of steel. He pulled Joseph's face close to his—close enough for Joseph to see the bits of spittle flying from his lips as he said, "I told you before to keep away. I warned you once. I told you what was gonna happen the next time I found your smelly ass snooping around . . ."

Shorty had twisted Joseph's collar so tight he could hardly breathe. "You got it wrong . . ." wheezed Joseph. But it was all he could get out. Shorty had thrown him up against the station wagon, slamming the back of his head hard against the window. Even through the pain, Joseph heard the crack of glass.

One fist came at him like a sledgehammer, hitting his abdomen, knocking out his air. Another hit his face, tearing open his lip. He could taste the warm rush of blood filling his mouth until Shorty's forearm came crashing down, striking him on the side of his neck. Then his lights went out.

The sweet odor of pine is what he smelled when he awoke. He saw a steamy mist before his eyes. Then he felt something moist against his face. He opened his eyes and saw a drooling tongue.

"Jesus bloody Christ!" Joseph shouted, shoving at the dog that was hovering over his face. "Get that slobbering mut away!"

Wolenski pushed the dog with his foot and held out the rag he had been using to sponge Joseph's wounds.

Joseph tried to sit up and felt the world spinning around him. He spat and noticed it was blood. Then grabbing the cloth from Wolenski's hand, he stuck it in his mouth and pulled out—a tooth.

"Fucking hell!" he muttered as he inspected it. "I don't even have dental insurance." Joseph looked up at the miserable man standing over him. "You could have helped."

Wolenski took the cloth and dipped it in the pine broth that was cooking on his alcohol stove. He squeezed out the excess fluid and then held it out again.

Joseph took the cloth and rubbed it over his aching face.

Wolenski meanwhile began packing up his stuff as Joseph struggled to his feet. Then, opening the door, he anxiously motioned for Joseph to slide himself in. The dog jumped into its pouch and Wolenski got behind the wheel. He started the Toyota and wasted no time sending it lurching down the street.

They drove down to the highway, shadowy in the evening light, and then back north again.

Joseph rubbed his jaw. "You think it'll swell?" he asked.

Wolenski gestured to the cloth and made daubing motions on his face.

"At least they didn't break my hands," said Joseph, wiggling his fingers and thinking what a pain it would be to write his next story with busted stumps.

Joseph turned to look at him. Wolenski was focusing on the road. The evening mist was heavy. He had turned the windshield wipers on, but it was still hard to see.

"I think there's a whole lot you're not telling me," said Joseph, aloud. "But don't bother to write it down."

The highway signs said they had reached the outskirts of Lake Oswego. Wolenski slowed down to thirty-five as the road ribboned through the shopping district and then out the other side.

Watching the rows of eateries pass by, each with their garish neon lights painting electrical swatches on the mist-drenched windscreen, he reconstructed in his mind the image of a bright red Jag parked in front of a roadhouse pub.

"Pull over," he said to Wolenski, who had stopped briefly for a light.

Wolenski looked at him questioningly as he started up again.

"Pull over!"

Wolenski slid over to the side of the road, stopped the car and looked at Joseph with a mixture of curiosity and dismay.

"Turn around and drive back to that roadhouse we just passed," said Joseph.

Wolenski did as he was told, but the expression on his face seemed to say, "If you wanted a drink, why didn't you ask?" He made a U-turn in front of a gigantic truck and drove back a hundred yards the way he came.

"Pull in there," said Joseph, pointing to a parking lot that was almost empty of cars except for two. One was a old Ford Pinto. The other, the red Jag.

Wolenski drove up by the Pinto and turned the engine off.

"Kill your lights," said Joseph. "You got a smoke?"

Wolenski turned off the headlights and then stared at Joseph as if he were mad.

"Do you have a cigarette?" Joseph repeated.

"Do you have a death wish?" Wolenski scribbled on his pad.

"Forget it," said Joseph, rolling the window down and staring at the red Jag. "Is that Tara's car?" he asked.

Wolenski shook his head.

"Well, McCullough's butler pointed her out to me. And that's the car she got into."

A light appeared in Wolenski's eyes. Then, quickly opening the driver's door, he got out, stepping briskly around the Jag and disappearing into the entrance of the pub.

After he left, Joseph searched through the pockets of his jacket till he found a half-smoked stub. One that Polly hadn't found.

Straightening it out, he lit up and then took a long satisfying, if somewhat guilty puff. His promise to her had been not to buy more cigarettes. He didn't actually promise not to smoke.

It was ten minutes later that he saw her. She had her arms around two guys. They were young. Probably in the military from the looks of their clothes and their haircuts. She was engaged in animated conversation. They were helping to hold her up.

He could see she was tipsy, even from a distance. How drunk wasn't exactly clear until she got close and said, in a giggling voice, for them to wait there while she went to throw up.

"Jesus!" the taller of the two guys said, as she fell against the side of the pub and began to retch. "Six drinks and she's had it!"

"Most broads are like that," said the other one. "They got a different metabolism." In the flashing light of the neon sign, Joseph could see that he was a fresh-faced kid with just a shadow of a moustache starting to sprout. "Drunk or sober, she's a looker, though, ain't she?"

"She sure is some classy bitch!" the taller one said, appreciatively.

Joseph took another puff at his cigarette and flicked the ember with his forefinger and then pocketing the stub, he made his way out. "Hey, fellas," he called out, walking up close to them. "I got a word of advice."

The two young guys looked at him in surprise. They clearly hadn't noticed someone else was there.

"Mind your business, buddy," said the fresh-faced kid with a growl.

"This is my business," said Joseph. "And I'd make tracks, if I were you."

"Who says?" asked the taller one, puffing out his chest like a bantam-weight gorilla.

"Any idea who her father is?"

It was a question that seemed to catch them off guard. "You know her dad?" asked the fresh-faced kid with the peach fuzz moustache.

"He's a pretty big man, hereabouts. He could lean on you hard." Joseph stepped forward so they could see his face.

Whatever they thought about his looks, his swollen face seemed to make some impression. "She picked us up, mister," said the taller guy, starting to back off.

"We were just helping her out," said the fresh-faced one.

Joseph nodded and gave them a knowing smile. "Sure. I understand."

"We couldn't just leave her here, mister," said the taller one. "Could we?"

"I'll tell you what," said Joseph. "You two vamoose, get it? Disappear. I'll see that she gets back."

They seemed happy to oblige. Maybe they figured they didn't want to end up with a face like that. Anyway, they got into their Pinto and took off.

She had finally stopped retching. During the commotion she had leaned herself against the wall of the pub and had slowly dropped bit by bit until she ended on her backside on the ground.

Joseph walked over and tried to help her regain the perpendicular.

"Get your hands off me, creep!" she shouted. "Who gave you the right to be my prison guard?"

"Nobody. OK? You're plastered. I'm just taking you home."

"The hell you are!" she shouted, working her way upright again. She took her purse and started bashing him over the head with it.

"Hey, back off, lady!" he hollered.

"You slimy bastard!" she yelled. "My father sent you, didn't he!" She walloped him again.

Even drunk, he thought she had a pretty good punch. He grabbed her arms and tried holding them behind her back. She bent down her head and bit his hand. At the same time, she reared back and kicked.

"Cut it out! I'm not working for your father!" He let go of her. She whirled around and swung at him again. This time she missed and landed, like a rag doll, on the asphalt. She started giggling.

He was sucking the gash she made on his hand as he looked at her lying on the ground, saliva dribbling from her drunken lips, giggling like a fool. She had looked so sophisticated when he had seen her just an hour or so before as she swished from her stately home into her Jaguar. He couldn't believe this was the same woman. He had half a mind to drive her to a lab and have her tested for rabies.

"Listen," he said, trying to regain his calm. "I'm not working for your dad. I met your father for the first time earlier today. I came with a friend of yours—Wolenski. He's inside the roadhouse looking for you right now . . ."

"Wolenski?" she started giggling hysterically again. "Who the hell is Wolenski?"

He looked at her strangely. "Aren't you Katherine?" he asked.

"Katherine? You idiot! I'm Camilla." Then her face suddenly darkened. "What do you want with my sister?"

"What happened to her?" asked Joseph, looking at the young woman intently.

"She got punished for being bad!" she said. And then she started giggling again.

"Who punished her, Camilla?"

"Stavos punished her," she laughed. "Stavos. Stavos punished her."

"Stavos who?" he asked.

"Stavos, Stavos, who is Stavos?" she kept on giggling. "Kathy is bad. Stavos is bad. Camilla is bad. Everyone's bad!" She looked up and tried to give him a sexy smile. "Except you. Who are you?"

"I'm Radkin. Joseph Radkin," he said, taking a card from his wallet and writing his hotel number on the back. "You're drunk as a skunk now, Camilla, but maybe you can remember my name."

"Joey," she laughed, twisting her head round and round as if it were the only way to make the world stop spinning.

"Yeah, Joey. Joey Radkin. I'm putting this card in your purse," he said, kneeling down and taking the purse that she had used to bash him with.

During the battering the catch had snapped open. Now the contents lay strewn over the ground. He methodically picked up all the baggage: lipstick, change purse, perfume, brush, condoms, pills . . .

66

He looked up and saw Wolenski. He seemed extremely confused.

"This is Katherine's sister, Camilla. Help me get her up," he said. He was flipping through her wallet: social security, credit cards up the gazzoo, driver's license—she was twenty-one and her middle name was Margo—address book . . .

She was still giggling like a fool. She pointed her finger at Wolenski. "Who are you, lover?" she asked. "Lover. Lover. Who are you?"

He flipped through the address book. A business card fell out. It lay on the ground face up in front of him. Wolenski reached down and picked it up. He stared at the business card a moment and his gangly body seemed to stiffen.

"Let me see that," said Joseph. Wolenski handed it to him. He read the name embossed on the paper: "Myron Stavos, MA".

Joseph slipped the card into his pocket. "Help me dump her in her car," he said to Wolenski.

They hauled her in together.

Joseph, who had never been in a Jaguar before, drove her back.

Chapter 9

He had managed to drive the Jag back to Dunthorp and then up the forested hills to the McCullough house. It wasn't easy, especially with Camilla McCullough spread out on his lap.

Wolenski had followed behind. Under protest—as if he felt one beating a night was enough.

Joseph wasn't anxious to wait around himself. He had parked the Jag by the iron gate and then, after pressing the button on the squawk box, had waited inside the station wagon until Haveck-the-butler had come out. Then they took off.

It was nearing eleven when Wolenski left Joseph at his hotel. The night clerk was perusing the late edition of the *Sporting News* and circling the underdogs at the Greyhound track as Joseph came over to pick up his key.

"There's also a message for you, sir," the night clerk said, handing him an envelope.

Joseph dropped the key in his pocket and inspected the envelope. It was sealed. There was no return address, just his name—"Mr Radkin"—and his room number scrawled across.

He tore it open and emptied the contents. It was a copy of yesterday's shipping report culled from the daily press. Just that. Nothing else.

"Do you know who sent this?" Joseph asked the night clerk.

The night clerk looked up at him from his racing form. "What is it?"

"A schedule of arrivals and departures for cargo ships," said Joseph, inspecting it again.

"Maybe someone wants to get you on a slow boat to China," the night clerk replied, circling a hundred to one shot in tomorrow's third race. Then, looking up at him again, he squinted his eyes. "But you look like you've been shanghaied already."

The two-seater bar in the lobby was just closing. Joseph managed to wangle a drink from the sleepy bartender—who looked at him as if he were something out of the black lagoon—and grabbed a cigarette from the bowl of freebies on the counter. He sat down on a stool, took a long drink from his glass of scotch and then lit up. The cigarette and whisky had a tranquilizing effect.

It was a while before he noticed his reflection in the mirrored wall on the other side of the bar. At first he thought it was a stranger. But then he realized that he was the only one sitting there.

His jaw was black and blue. One side of his face was starting to puff up. He rubbed it gently. It still hurt. He reached into the pocket of his shirt and found his tooth. Holding it between his thumb and forefinger, he opened his mouth and tried fitting it back in. Somehow the gap had widened. He wondered whether crazy glue would work.

He put the tooth back in his shirt, finished his drink and stubbed his cigarette out, half-consciously slipping the butt into his pocket to have for the next day. Then he walked up the stairs with the shabby rug to the second floor.

Opening the door to his room and turning on the lights, he walked over to the TV and flipped through the channels until he found one that had the evening news. Ignoring the litany of murders and bludgeonings, he left it on while he went into the closet-like loo to brush his teeth—or what was left of them.

". . . here at home," the announcer was saying, "the forest issue has become focused on the Bear Creek region of the Cascades . . ."

Joseph came back into the room, the toothbrush in his hand and traces of foamy paste oozing from his mouth.

On screen was an aerial shot of a massive forest. ". . . these ancient Hemlock and Douglas fir, some seven to eight hundred years old, are what the dispute is about. Whether the forest will survive . . ."

The screen suddenly came alive with bulldozers and cranes,

smashing their way through the woods. ". . . or fall to the lumber companies . . ."

A close-up of a lumber industry spokesman, dressed in a hard yellow hat, plaid jacket and overalls, came on. ". . . the question is whether we want our sawmills to become historic sites or if we wish to maintain them as a vital part of our economy. Well over five thousand of our household products come from trees and the Pacific Northwest provides half of the nation's harvestable timber. The wood products industry is responsible for forty-four percent of Oregon's economy. Second growth forests on private timber stands won't be physically mature for twenty to thirty years. Old growth on federally held land is still 7.5 million acres. Frankly, if we want to keep our people employed and our economy humming, there is no alternative available . . .'

The shot switched to a close-up of a pair of giant blinking eyes peering from a feathered head. ". . . up till now the cutting of Bear Creek Forest has been enjoined thanks to a bird. The spotted owl. Protected under the endangered species act, naturalists fear the rare birds could disappear in twenty to forty years if their nesting places in old growth stands continue to be cut down . . ."

A close-up of a professorial man standing in a woody glen came on. ". . . The forests are almost gone. Unfortunately, most people in America have no idea what is happening. It's not a question of the spotted owl or a fox or a rare flower—an entire ecosystem is being dismembered. The environmental consequences of this disaster go far beyond the survival of a bird. It has implications for the whole of the human race . . ."

The screen lit up with the image of Meade College. ". . . that was Dr Nathaniel Bright, one of the spokesmen for Environmental Action. Professor Bright, who died at his faculty residence at Meade College yesterday, was also concerned about one of the by-products of the timber industry . . ."

Suddenly a massive factory appeared on screen, smokestacks spewing out clouds of darkness. In the background, rows of logs were propelled down the rushing waters.

". . . dioxin. Considered one of the most deadly toxins

known to man, dioxin has been found in the effluent of most paper plants that is flushed into our rivers . . ."

Now came a tight shot of a severe-looking bald-headed man in a business suit. Joseph thought he looked very much like the fellow he had seen at McCullough's house earlier that day.

"Mr Charles Martin is vice-president of McCullough Paper Company . . ." the narrator said, before Martin's voice came on.

"It's true that dioxin has been found in traceable quantities in the effluent of the bleaching process during the manufacture of paper, but the effects of dioxin in minuscule quantities—in our case 222 parts per quadrillion—has never been proven harmful to humans. It must be emphasized that dioxin is found naturally as the consequence of spontaneous combustion . . ."

The close-up shifted to a man in a laboratory jacket standing in front of a blackboard, holding a pointer in his hand. On the blackboard was the drawing of a factory dumping its waste into a stream. In the stream were snails and fish. Floating above was a fisherman in his boat.

"However Paul Kessler of Scientific Data finds even these trace amounts unsettling . . ."

". . . chlorine waste containing dioxin and furan is dumped into the water," Kessler said, moving his pointer, "where the minute particles settle on the bottom. The toxins enter the food chain through tiny creatures like snails which graze on the effluent. Small fish eat the polluted insects and crustaceans. Larger fish, like trout, then eat the smaller fish. Humans eat the trout, accumulating the dioxin and furan in their fatty tissues. These have the potential to cause birth defects and immune system disorders . . ."

The screen filled with mist. There was a roaring sound and the magnificent view of a gigantic waterfall. The camera panned to a small blockhouse perched on a mid-river island set very close to the falls. The blockhouse was surrounded by a high fence of barbed wire.

"A half mile upstream from their main plant, McCullough Paper has built a prototype of their new bleaching machinery that they hope will change all this by turning paper white without the creation of dioxin or furan. The day after tomorrow, the permit committee of DEQ meets to rule on plans for a new paper mill proposed by McCullough. The plant will cost one half billion dollars to construct and will provide employment for over one thousand Oregonians. However, there's a catch . . ."

The picture was now of a female newscaster, a young woman dressed in stylish ski clothes standing in a forest clearing.

"The catch is," she said, motioning a mittened hand to the majestic trees behind her, "if the paper mill is built then all this might go. McCullough Lumber, which has cutting rights to Bear Creek, is a subsidiary of McCullough Paper. Sources close to the industry say that a new pulp mill will cost nearly a half billion dollars—quite a hunk of cash."

She turned around to the dense forest. "But there's gold in those hills behind me. In recent years these huge trees have found a ready market in the lumber-starved nations of the Far East—countries like Japan which use them as raw material to make finished products that they sell back to us again. The Japanese will pay two thousand dollars for each prime old growth fir out there. That works out to about one hundred thousand dollars an acre. McCullough Lumber holds cutting rights to thirty-one thousand acres of old growth forest. And that adds up to a lot of numbers!"

The picture switched to a long shot of a gigantic office building, a post-modern monstrosity with a lot of glass and turquoise.

"The headquarters of McCullough Industries in downtown Portland has been the scene of much activity in the last several days." The camera panned in on a slick-haired man with a thick moustache holding on to a microphone.

"James McCullough, president of McCullough Paper held a press conference earlier today with Mr Henry Mellon, chief counsel for Oregon Wilderness Commission where an agreement was announced of a one year's moratorium on cutting Bear Creek. This agreement was reached in exchange for OWC's support of McCullough's new pulp paper mill . . ."

The screen showed an excerpt of the film footage from the press conference. McCullough was shaking hands with Mellon, who Joseph now realized was the man he had seen walking out of Abigail's house earlier that day.

It cut to an interview with McCullough.

"As a native Oregonian, whose family helped build the northwest, there's no one more concerned than I about the preservation of our forests and our wildlife. I think the agreement that we reached today with our friends in the conservationist movement goes a long way toward protecting our wilderness as well as giving us the economic impetus to revitalize our industrial base . . ."

The footage cut to Mellon. He was all smiles. "I think we've shown here today how it's possible for industry and environmentalists to work together to protect our wilderness and, at the same time, create jobs and keep our economy strong. There are no villains in this story. We all want the same thing. It's just a matter of having the patience to sort things out . . ."

The station cut to a break, promising that if you held on through the commercials they'd throw you some sports and weather. Joseph pulled the plug and watched the screen go black.

He finished rinsing his mouth and then, undoing his shoes, he slipped them off and went to bed.

Chapter 10

His phone rang promptly at 7.00 a.m. It jarred him from his strange dreams of hanging out with the apes in the woods. He reached over and answered it:

"Got some interesting news for you to start your day," came a voice he recognized. "You ready?"

Joseph pushed a hand through some unruly hair and sat up in bed. "Depends on what position you want me in."

"I talked to a friend of mine in forensics. Seems Bright was killed all right . . ." Nickels' voice sounded almost cheerful.

"Are they sure?" Joseph was holding the phone under his chin while attempting to put his shoes on.

"Seems pretty sure—unless he killed himself by bashing in his own head."

"Someone killed him by clubbing him on the head?"

"My source claims he was beaten to a pulp."

Joseph was putting on his socks. "So why put a lid on it? I thought the dailies thrive on gruesome murders . . ."

"You might as well ask why the police are tiptoeing around this case . . ."

"Why?" He figured he knew. He just wanted to hear Nickels say it.

"The powers that be want to cool things off—at least till the permit hearings are over. Someone's got his pudgy finger in the dike, even though they can't hold back the waters for long. But till the day after tomorrow? I'd say yes."

"I thought things had cooled down," said Joseph, giving a final tug to a recalcitrant shoe. "I saw a bit of that press conference with ecology and business patting each other on the back—seems it was all hugs and smiles."

"Yeah, well that was a nice show, wasn't it? Even more remarkable considering what was left out . . ."

"What was left out?"

"Certain facts, such as the moratorium concerned only clear cutting—going into Bear Creek and ripping out all the trees. They can still engage in selective harvesting . . ."

"Meaning?"

"McCullough Lumber can still cut parts of the forest any time they damn well please. Anyway, there's nothing written, just promises without any legal binding. And the promises are so riddled with qualifications that they really aren't worth much."

"So why the agreement?"

"Because the Wilderness Commission needed something that looked like a victory. And maybe they'll gain from it— who knows? Maybe they've got some leverage where they hadn't before. I mean the bulk of the forests are going to be cut down one way or another. Everyone knows that. I guess they hope to save a little bit. And maybe this guy McCullough is on the square. Maybe he really is a closet conservationist."

Joseph was on his way out when the young woman with bright eyes behind the registration desk called out to him.

"Mr Radkin? There's a message for you, sir."

He walked over to the desk and she handed him a folded slip of paper. He opened it up. "Tara may be in great danger. I think Myron Stavos knows what happened to her," the message read.

"Who left this for me?" Joseph asked the clerk.

She pointed a charming finger in the direction of the tiny lounge. "That man over there."

Wolenski was sound asleep in an easy chair.

"How long has he been here?" asked Joseph.

"Since early this morning." She looked at Joseph strangely.

"Anything wrong?" he asked.

"No . . . it's just your . . ." She touched her cheek.

He glanced at himself in the mirror behind the registration desk. One side of his face was swollen and discolored.

"It's nothing," he said, turning back to her with a forced

smile. "It gets like that sometimes." Then, walking over to where Wolenski was dozing, he put a hand on his shoulder and gave him a shake. "Time to wake up, sleeping beauty," he said.

Wolenski's eyes popped open and his body tensed.

Joseph held out the note the clerk had just given him. "What's the meaning of this?" he asked.

Stretching his skinny arms and then rubbing his eyes, Wolenski reached into his pocket for his pad.

"Make it short," said Joseph pulling out the card that he had taken from Camilla's purse last night. "What do you know about this Stavos character?"

"Stavos calls himself a deprogrammer," Wolenski scribbled. "He makes his living saving kids from cults."

"What's this got to do with Tara?" asked Joseph.

Tearing off a sheet from his pad, Wolenski continued. "Stavos was one of the last people she interviewed."

"For the article on right-wing cults?"

His pencil started up again. "I saw the card her sister dropped last night."

"You mean this one," said Joseph, holding it out.

Wolenski nodded. "I need your help," he wrote. "What's the address?"

"Shark Street," said Joseph, handing the card to him.

Shark Street might not have been exactly in skid row, but it was close. There wasn't a true demarcation line where the drunks stopped and bean sprout sandwiches began, just a vague transition in the morning litter from empties of cheap wine to those of Perrier water.

Number 17 was a four-story dilapidated brick building with an old fashioned wire-cage elevator that didn't work. They climbed the stairs to the second floor and then walked down the hall till they came to a door of wavy glass with a sign that read, MYRON STAVOS, MA. Through the fun-house effect of the corrugation, they could see a silhouette that curled up like writhing snakes.

"Wait outside," said Joseph, giving his shadow a significant look.

Wolenski shrugged.

Joseph gave a knock.

The writhing snakes became one and the silhouette straightened out. A voice which had the quality of sandpaper said, "Come in."

Joseph pulled the door open and walked inside. A middle-aged woman with saggy features, dull eyes and brittle hair looked at him somewhat questioningly, as if she wondered why he was there but didn't really care too much.

"Is Mr Stavos in?" asked Joseph, giving her a professional smile.

The woman had a cigarette dangling from her lips. It jiggled up and down as she answered him. "Who wants to know?"

Taking the card that Camilla McCullough had given him, he showed it to her. "A friend of mine gave me this. He thought that Mr Stavos could help me out."

She squinted her eyes. Some ash from her cigarette fell on her desk. "You got a kid in trouble?"

"Maybe," he said.

"Girl or boy?"

"Does it matter?"

"It matters," she said. "Boys can put up more of a fight. But they're easier to fix." She smiled thinly with her lips, not with her eyes, and showed him her tobacco-stained teeth. "You know what I mean?"

"You mean girls are more stubborn."

"They can be." She looked down at a large date book on her desk and turned the page. "I can set you up an appointment with Mr Stavos, but not till next week."

Joseph shook his head. "Too late," he said.

"If it's an emergency, I'll have to contact him." She took a pen in her left hand and looked up at him. "What's your name?"

"Radkin. Joseph Radkin."

"What's the name of your kid?"

"I've got two of them. Tanya and Abe. They're twins."

"Twins? That's a new one! How old are they?"

"Five."

She put down her pen. "What's this all about, mister?"

"It's not my kids. It's someone else's."

She stared at him suspiciously. "Are you a reporter?"

"I'm a journalist. I'd like to speak with Mr Stavos about Katherine McCullough."

He could see her face suddenly tense up. "Mr Stavos don't speak to reporters, Mister!" she said. "And he don't allow me to neither!"

"Is that because he's afraid?" asked Joseph. "Kidnapping is a serious crime, isn't it. Even in this state . . ."

She made herself look busy, trying to ignore him.

"There's also an associated offense known as conspiracy to kidnap. You don't have to be involved in the actual kidnapping to be charged. Get my drift?"

The point of her pencil broke, she was bearing down on it so hard. Her face finally had some expression in it as she looked up at him in anger. "You don't know what you're talking about! When your kids become Moonies or Hari Krishna freaks, then maybe you'll come crawling back here on your hands and knees . . ."

"How about if they become ecologists?" he asked.

"How about if they become terrorists?" she spat. "Get out of here, Mister!" She picked up the receiver of the telephone. "Or do you want me to call the cops."

He shrugged. "Go ahead and call them. I'm sure they'd be interested in knowing about your little scam."

"Get out of here!" she shouted. She threw her broken pencil at him.

"Tell Stavos I was here," he said, giving her a wave. And then he left. He wasn't going to wait around for her to throw the typewriter.

Wolenski had parked about a block away. When Joseph came down, he pulled into the yellow zone across the street from the dilapidated brick building and waited.

Sooner than he thought, the woman from Stavos' office walked out of the front entrance. She hesitated when she reached the sidewalk, glancing quickly to her right and then to her left, before she hurriedly made her way down an alley that led to the rear of the building and turned right, out of their line of sight, into a parking lot.

"Next car that you see come out," said Joseph.

It was a white Ford Escort. He could see her face clearly through the windscreen.

"Follow her," he told Wolenski. "Keep three cars behind."

Wolenski made a daring U-turn in front of a moving bus.

Joseph closed his eyes and then quickly opened them again. He pointed. "She turned right!"

They followed her over a bridge and then north along a large thoroughfare. She drove for about three or four miles and then made a left.

It was a run-down area. Half the shops were boarded up. The other half looked like they were soon going to be.

A big sign scrawled across a peeling stucco wall said, "No more Crack or Meth-amphetamines!"

She had turned right without putting on her signal and then turned right again.

Suddenly a truck pulled out in front of them. Wolenski squealed to a stop.

He threw the wagon into reverse and tried to go around. By the time he made the turn, the Ford Escort was gone.

"Try cruising down some of the side streets," Joseph suggested.

Wolenski criss-crossed several neigborhood roads. They found the Escort on a street named Lilly, parked in front of 1789.

It looked like the rest of the neighboring buildings which still stood in this war zone. Except this one was securely surrounded by a chain link fence that was about ten feet in height and topped with wire which looked as if it was sharp as razor. A sign on the fence had a picture of something huge, dark and saber-toothed, along with the word, BEWARE! At the side of the house was a kennel with some snarling things that were clearly to be bewared about.

Wolenski gave him a look which seemed to question whether they should stay or take off to safer shores. Joseph motioned for him to drive the wagon around the block.

The view from the corner wasn't bad. He could see Stavos'

79

front yard through the gaps in the burned-out edifice that was blighting the last parcel of land at the corner of the street.

They had been parked there for about twenty minutes, Joseph puffing on his last stub of a cigarette and Wolenski sipping some camomile tea and keeping upwind from the noxious fumes. At about half-past ten, the front door opened and a hulking man stepped out on the porch. He wore a black leather jacket and cowboy boots. He stood there for a moment, glancing around. Then he went back inside, leaving open the door.

Joseph motioned to Wolenski to let him out of the car.

A minute later, now standing behind a hedge, Joseph saw a slender man, white-haired, not more than five foot five come out followed by the woman from the Shark Street office. She was wearing a white uniform and was holding on to the arm of a young woman, a brunette with long flowing hair, who wore a loose-fitting polka-dot dress.

"Is that Katherine?" asked Joseph. He glanced at Wolenski, who was standing by the car.

By the time Wolenski came forward to get a closer look, the small, white-haired man had already started to open the gate.

Joseph bounded over to him.

"Mr Stavos!" he waved his hand and shouted. "Mr Stavos! I'd like to talk to you . . ."

Stavos looked over at him in surprise. The woman in the white uniform stared in Joseph's direction, icily, while clutching the young woman, whose arm she held securely with both hands—gripping it even tighter than before. The young woman also glanced up, though without much interest, before looking down, listlessly, at the ground again.

He was about twenty feet from them when he saw the hulking man in the black jacket and cowboy boots running down the path which led from the house.

"I'd just like to ask you a few questions—I'm a journalist . . ." Joseph said, quickly trying to establish his credentials before all hell broke loose.

The woman in the white uniform pushed the young girl into the back seat of the Ford as Stavos turned to Joseph and looked at him with disdain. "I don't talk to reporters," he said.

"I want to know about Katherine McCullough, Mr Stavos," Joseph continued, talking fast. He pointed to the back seat of the Ford where the young woman was quietly sitting. "Is that her in there?"

"Lester!" Stavos shouted looking over at the house.

Joseph glanced in that direction, himself, and saw two huge black dobermans, barking like banshees, foam dripping from their mouths, spring from their kennel and make for the gate which Lester was holding wide open.

"Bloody hell!" Joseph shouted. For a second he was frozen in place. But just for a second. Then he began running for his life. He headed for the station wagon, shouting "Wolenski! Open the goddam door!"

Wolenski, however, was still by the hedge, and when he saw Joseph coming, he turned and scrambled up the car onto the roof. Holding out his hand, he grabbed onto Joseph's arm and helped lift him up, out of the jaws of the snarling beasts.

There they stood on top of the old rusty Toyota as the dogs howled and leapt just inches from their feet while back at the house the man in the leather jacket shook his head, crossed one cowboy boot over the other, chewed down on the toothpick in his mouth and grinned.

Wolenski's little mut peeked out his pocket and made a mouse-like squeak.

With Stavos at the wheel, the Ford Escort took off.

Chapter 11

Wolenski dropped him back at his hotel after Lester had called off the hounds enabling them to scramble through the one usable door of the Toyota again. Joseph said he'd call him later.

It wasn't Katherine in the car. Wolenski had confirmed that by giving Joseph a copy of a photograph. It was a picture of them both standing in front of a giant tree. She had smiling blue eyes and facial muscles that pulled the sides of her mouth in a downward direction, like a young Greta Garbo, giving her an air of mystery. She was gazing at the camera as if it weren't there. Wolenski was looking at her. It was a different Wolenski though. His face seemed relaxed. He looked almost happy.

Joseph was lost in that photographic image when he opened the hotel door and collided with her as she was coming out. Her hat fell from her head.

"Sorry," he said, as he reached down to retrieve it. "I'm a little off kilter today. Some hounds from Baskerville just tried tearing me to shreds."

She gave him a pretty smile. "That's OK," she said. "I'm always bumping into people myself and I don't even have an excuse."

Picking up his key, the clerk at the registration desk handed him another envelope. This one contained a card for the Park Lane Hotel. On the back of the card was written a room number.

"Who left this for me?" Joseph asked the clerk.

"A young woman," she said. "Just a few seconds before you walked in."

"What did she look like?"

"Casual. Petite . . ."

Joseph took out the photo Wolenski had given him. "Is this her?" he asked, showing it to the clerk.

She shook her head. "I couldn't say. I really didn't see her face. I was on the phone. She said your name and walked away. All I saw was her bright red beret . . ."

He raced out the door again and saw her strolling down the grassy area that divided the road. She was several blocks up from him when she crossed the road and headed toward an open path between two buildings.

The path led to the side entrances of the Northwest Film Center on the right and the Art Museum on the left. A bearded black man standing behind an outdoor espresso stand on wheels stared at him as he came puffing up.

"A young woman . . ." Joseph said, pointing to his head.

The man behind the espresso stand made his eyes into saucers and pointed to his own kinky hair.

". . . wearing a red beret . . ." Joseph gestured anxiously with his hands.

The man gestured back like a mime mimicking his shadow.

"Short, slim, young, red beret. Here just a second ago. Did you see where she went?"

"Short, slim, young, red beret. Here just a second ago. Did I see where she went?"

Joseph stared at the man and ground his teeth. He took a dollar out of his wallet and slapped it down on the counter. "Gimme an espresso!" he growled.

The man pressed out an espresso and handed it to him in a little paper cup. He smiled. "Try the art school, man," he said.

Joseph swallowed the coffee in one gulp and hurried through the glass doors that led to the art school. The hall was empty.

"Any classes just starting?" he asked, running up to the elderly woman sitting at the information desk.

She looked at him curiously.

He gave her a silly grin. "My girlfriend. She forgot her diaphragm . . .'

She didn't react but pointed down the narrow passageway. "Life drawing. Second on your left."

83

Maybe its a common situation these days, he thought, as he raced down the hall.

He pulled open the door and barged into the room. About a dozen young women were stationed at their easels, surrounding a naked Adonis standing on a pedestal and showing off his muscle tone.

The look of surprise on Joseph's face prompted a few giggles.

He quickly glanced around the room. All the girls looked the same to him, slim and artsy. None were wearing a red beret.

But he was here and already as embarrased as he was likely to get. So, clearing his throat, he said, "Did anyone drop off an envelope at the Cambridge Arms today?"

The response to his words were confused looks and stony silence.

"Well, have a nice day," he said. Then he walked out.

He was halfway to the reception desk when he heard someone call. "Hey, mister!"

Turning, he saw the young woman wearing the red hat.

"Did you want to see me?" she asked.

"Are you Katherine?" he said, walking back to where she was standing.

"No. My name's Melody." The pretty smile he had seen before was back on her face.

He pulled out the card for the Park Lane Hotel from his pocket and showed it to her. "What's this?"

She shrugged. "Beats me," she said.

"But you left it for me!"

"Yeah, but I didn't know what it was . . ."

"Gimme a break, sister!"

"I was having a sandwich on the park bench right outside the museum when this guy comes up to me and offers ten bucks if I'll leave an envelope for you. I said not if it's drugs. He says it's just a note. I said why don't you bring it yourself. He says he's your dad and he doesn't want to embarrass you. So I say I can dig that . . .'

"My dad?"

"That's what he said."

He stared at her. "But that's impossible!" said Joseph.

"Why?" she asked. "Dads do things like that . . ."

"Except that my dad's dead," he said.

The Cambridge Arms had a tired look to it, he thought glancing down at the fraying carpet underneath his feet as he walked up the stairs. It wasn't quite shabby, not yet, at least. But it was well on its way.

He didn't know why he felt a tingling sensation in the small of his back when he took the key and inserted it into the lock. It could have been the disinfectant spray that often got up his nose when he stayed in hotels. It set off an allergic reaction which began like that. It was a queasy feeling that made him break out in cold sweats. If he had his choice, he would have opted for the germs which tended to co-exist with the pollutants in his body much better than that dank protective spray.

On the other hand, the side of his face was hurting again where he had been slugged. He used the tip of his tongue to probe the narrow space in his mouth which his tooth had vacated the other day and decided that the tingling sensation had more to do with a general aura of vague disgust than over-used chemicals.

Pushing open the door he walked in and then closed it behind him. He went over to the bed and lay down and looked up at the ceiling, allowing himself to drift through the images and notions vying for space in his brain.

The image which predominated was of a young woman, barely more than a girl—the one he had seen that morning in Stavos' car. With her long, flowing hair and her wide eyes—so innocent, so drugged—she looked like any flower child on pot. Except she didn't have that air of wonder and of awe, of reaching out to touch another universe. And the drug that made her eyes so expressionless wasn't pot—he was sure of that—but something much more sinister.

Twenty years before he might have seen her in the Haight. The parks in San Francisco had been filled to the brim with kids like her in the sixties. Not anymore. Now the parks were filled with a different breed. More abject, much more hopeless, without even the pretense of ideals.

And he wondered where all the flower children had gone.

Gone to Stavos, every one? Deprogrammed? Defantasized? Reconstructed into good upstanding citizens?

Or perhaps they had taken refuge in the forest?

And then there was the guy who said he was his father. What the hell was that all about? he wondered.

He sat up in bed and pulled out the card he had stuck in his pocket. Then he reached for the phone.

He placed a call to the Park Lane Hotel and asked for room 331.

The operator connected him at once. He heard the sound of voices in the background. A heated discussion was going on. Then a female voice said: "Can I help you?"

"Who is this?" asked Joseph.

"This is Mr Tobias' secretary. I'm sorry he can't come to the phone right now . . ." The voices in the background were growing louder. It didn't seem to him like an argument exactly, but the voices were intent. "Can I take a message?"

"Someone left me a card with your room number," said Joseph. "I gather whoever it was expected me to call."

"Perhaps if you gave me some reference . . ."

"My name is Radkin. Joseph Radkin."

"And you wanted to speak with someone at Millennium Investments?"

"Someone wanted to speak with me, I think . . ." He looked at the card again. Perhaps the "1" was a "7". "Unless I have the wrong room."

"Maybe you do," she said.

He replaced the call to the Park Lane and spoke with the clerk at reception.

"Could you tell me who you have registered in room 337?" Joseph asked.

"I'm sorry," the clerk replied, "but it's not our policy to give out that information. However, I can tell you that the third floor is off limits to guests this week."

"Off limits?" asked Joseph.

"Yes. All the rooms have been block-booked by an organization. They have private meetings going on."

He hung up the telephone and rubbed an itchy spot under his nose.

What the hell was going on? he wondered. Why was some-one trying to lead him to the Park Lane Hotel?

On the other hand, he thought, he wasn't being paid to find that out, was he? He was being paid to find out about the new pulp paper mill—for purposes Saunders had kept to himself.

There was a strange taste in his mouth. Somehow all of this didn't feel right. But there it was. He had sold his professional skills to someone for purposes that he could only guess. And why? Perhaps because it was politic to accept an assignment from a member of the board even if West had said it was up to him. In fact, at first West had even tried to discourage him from taking it. He said he had a magazine to run and couldn't have his staff off running errands. It was only after the accountant had pointed out the huge deficit *Investigations* had built up over the year that West had changed his tune. And if one of the money bags needed something done in exchange for feeding the kitty, well, Radkin, maybe . . ."

So much for principle, Radkin thought. And you better not think about the implications.

He went over to the writing table and opened the folder that contained the material on McCullough Paper that Nickels had given him and paged through the xeroxed articles from the past issues of the newspaper dated back some thirty years.

The story that unfolded was slightly different from the one he had set up in his head. The industry—according to the clippings—had suffered through some bad times. A while back the lumber business was close to collapse. Logging had ceased. Mills had closed. Lumberjacks and mill workers were standing in breadlines. Houses were abandoned. The population of the state had actually decreased.

Things eventually got better after they couldn't get any worse. But in the course of the "recession" many smaller companies went broke. In fact, according to an article he read, you could have counted on your fingers the ones that survived.

McCullough Lumber had toughed it out and entered the decade of affluence in fighting shape. He wondered how.

He give Nickels a call. They traced him to a desk in the City Room.

"What's this business about a fire at the McCullough lumber mill a number of years back?" Joseph asked.

"Pretty big blaze from what I remember," Nickels replied.

"How come it didn't shut them down?"

"Everyone was shut down in those days, Radkin . . ."

"No, I mean, they seem to have survived the loss OK."

"Did you ever hear of insurance?"

Joseph let that sink in. Then he asked, "By the way, did you send me a shipping report the other day?"

"What's that again?"

"You know, the daily column on the port activities."

"Not likely."

"Well somebody did. And there aren't many people who know me up here—or my digs. Then today I get another envelope—hand delivered, mind you. Inside is a card for the Park Lane Hotel . . ."

"Maybe someone's suggestion that you move to a better part of town—by ship."

"I called the room number written on the back and was hooked up with an outfit that calls itself Millennium Investments. Ever heard of them?"

"Nope. But a lot of these financial groups are like free-floating atoms. Always looking for a molecule to bond with. They change names faster than a movie starlet. I'll ask the editor at the business desk what he knows."

"Thanks," said Joseph. "I'll call you later." And he hung up the phone.

He reached into his jacket pocket in hopes of finding one of the cigarette butts he had saved. Instead he found the tabloid Wolenski had given him—*The Midnight Special*.

Paging through, he stopped to read the editorial:

"Over the last twenty years, Oregon has been seeing the last of its old growth forests cut down—ancient forests that formed an ecosystem that took over two thousand years to evolve. And why? To create jobs? Doesn't it seem somewhat ironic that the more trees we cut, the fewer jobs we have? Maybe we should be asking ourselves how many jobs there will be left after the last tree is gone? Timber has sustained Oregon for most of its history, but, as many Third World countries now understand, there comes a time when natural resources run out. And then it's too late to ask what you have sacrificed for a moonscape of stumps. The time to ask that question is now. So—how much are we prepared to sacrifice to keep mill owners fat? Wilderness? Wildlife? Clean water? Fish in our streams? Millionaire lumbermen don't give a damn about their workers or our land. I, for one, will never let them destroy what remains of our ancient forests. They will never get Bear Creek! They must be stopped!"

He turned back to the front page article, the one written by Tara about the supposed relationship of a right-wing cult group with the timber industry. It was one of those articles that was filled with tumult and shouting but ending up saying nothing at all. Supposedly the cult provided the money and manpower for a front group which was promoting the continued exploitation of the wilderness in order to provide wealth and jobs.

So bloody what? he thought. Propaganda is propaganda whether it comes from right, left or center. It could be funded by cults or the Republican National Committee. The article was a perfect example of a non-story masquerading as news. If that's what Wolenski was teaching her, no wonder she cut out.

The swelling on the side of his face began to hurt. He tried to ignore it.

So where was this getting him, he wondered. OK, so maybe Tara found something out. But what would Stavos want with her? He probably was in enough trouble with all the suits and legal injunctions piling up against him. Why would he mess with some influential rich guy's kid? Unless . . .

The telephone rang. He picked it up.

"Mr Radkin?" It was a woman's voice. Self-assured, but slightly apprehensive. "This is Abigail Bright."

"What can I do for you?" he asked.

"There's something I'd like to talk with you about. I wonder if you might come over to my place—at your convenience, of course . . ."

Slipping on his shoes with his free hand, he said, "My convenience? Sure! How about now?"

Chapter 12

He took a cab to the Overton Street house. As he walked up to the porch, he noticed the curtains of the window were pulled back. He saw her sitting in an easy chair. A book was on her lap. She wasn't reading, however, as the book was closed. She seemed to be deep in thought.

Joseph knocked on the door. Gently—for him. A soft patter rather than a boisterous rat-a-tat-tat.

Through the window, he saw her reaction. She was expecting him, but, even so, she seemed startled.

She went to the door and let him in.

"It was kind of you to come," she said, ushering him into the living room.

"It's my job," he said, sitting in the same place on the couch where he had sat the day before. "I come when I'm called. Sort of like Mighty Mouse. Remember him?" He looked at her and grinned.

"Actually, not," she replied, "I grew up in Europe." She was fidgeting with something in her hand. It seemed to him that her mind was someplace else. Her eyes were looking beyond him.

"You wanted to speak with me," he reminded her.

She suddenly returned from wherever she had drifted. He could tell it by her eyes; they were now focused directly on him. "It was about yesterday—I hadn't understood yet . . ."

"Understood what?"

"That my father had been murdered." She turned around as she said it so he couldn't see her face. "I was prepared for him to die—but not like that."

"Have you seen the autopsy report?" he asked.

"No."

"The police didn't need you to identify the body?"

"Someone at his college . . ." she began and then she stopped.

He figured she didn't know the worst—that her father's head had been bashed to a pulp—and he didn't want to be the one to tell her.

Her eyes were red when she turned around again. "My friends have suggested that I let the police get on with their job and leave it at that."

"Possibly a good suggestion," replied Joseph. "Have they been around to interview you yet?"

"Not yet."

"I'm sure they'll get around to it. They've got a lot of things to do."

"Yes. I'm sure they'll see me—after the pulp mill hearing." She gave him a significant look. "I'm afraid I wasn't totally frank with you yesterday . . ."

"Sometimes I'm not totally frank with people either. It's not a crime."

"You see there was some information that my father had obtained. Something he was sure would prevent the new pulp mill from being built and save the Bear Creek Forest . . ."

She stood up and walked over to a desk at the side of the room. Opening a small drawer, she pulled something out. Then she turned back to him. "I suppose he felt that whoever had this information could possibly come to some harm. He didn't want to endanger me, but at the same time he made it quite clear he knew something that could have an enormous influence . . ."

"You mean he was involved in blackmail."

She stared at him for a moment before she spoke, as if she, herself, were trying to figure something out. "I'm not sure I'd call it that. It was more political . . ."

"All politics are a form of blackmail, in some degree or other," he said. "But I won't quibble with you. This information—it pertained to the permit hearing I suppose . . ."

"I had the distinct impression that whatever he found out had come to him quite recently."

"But you have no idea why or how."

She shook her head. "However several days before . . ." She made a visible effort to control herself. ". . . before his death, I received this in the mail."

She had an envelope in her hand from which she removed a slip of paper. She held it out.

Joseph stood and took the slip of paper from her hand. There was only one word written in bold caps: "POLISTES".

"Do you know what this means?" Joseph asked.

"No. But I do remember my father telling me once about an organization he was in. A small group of young men that met some years ago at Stanford. They called themselves the Papyrus Club. He referred to one of the men in the club as Polistes. I remember because it's such a curious name."

Joseph took out the notebook from his jacket and wrote a few things down. "I'd like to ask you some questions," he said.

"Why don't we go into the kitchen," she suggested. "I'll make something to drink."

He followed her down the woody hall past leafy plants and woven wall hangings to the room in the back. It was a large kitchen with lots of light. A glass dormer extended from the rear wall giving a greenhouse effect. A rectangular teak dining table was set inside the space it provided.

"Very nice," said Joseph, sitting down at the table at her request.

"Yes, I do love this room," she said. She said it with sort of a sigh. "This was my parents' house. When my mother died and my father moved into the cottage, he gave it to me. But the kitchen is my design."

She offered him some coffee which she made in a pressurized contraption. She also set out a plate of cheeses, breads and condiments.

"So what made you decide to tell me all this?" he asked her as he helped himself a sandwich.

"I had a feeling about you," she said.

He looked up from his sandwich. She was staring at him.

"What kind of a feeling?"

"A feeling that you might be able to help. One needs to work on trust, don't you think. Otherwise, what's left?"

He took a bite of his sandwich. It tasted good. He wasn't crazy about cheese. Maybe it was the mustard.

"What's left isn't much," he said, wiping his mouth with the napkin she was kind enough to give him, "but it usually is all there was in the first place." He sort of smiled. "What is it you want me to help you with?"

"Help me find out what happened to my father."

"Have you discussed this with anyone else?"

"Only Henry."

"You mean the guy I saw here last time. The one who made the deal with McCullough."

She seemed to blush, though very slightly. "Yes. Henry Mellon."

He made a half sandwich figuring another whole one would be too much. "I'll be straight with you, too," he said. "I'm down here for only a few days to pick up as much information as I can as fast as I can pick it. But I'm not picking up a lot. And what I have picked up doesn't make a lot of sense. There are too many threads, too many tangents. They all seem to be going in different directions and I'm not really sure they're coming from the same center. Your father interests me and I'd certainly like to find out what happened to him. But I don't know how much time I can spend."

"Perhaps my father's information could help tie it together for you," she said.

"The problem with your father's information is that it isn't here," he replied, giving her an apologetic look.

"I'm sure that message he sent me means something," she said.

"Maybe it does," he replied. "Maybe it doesn't."

"There's a photograph, I recall . . ."

"A photograph of what?"

She looked at him again. She had lovely eyes, he thought. He was always a sucker for lovely eyes.

"A photograph of the members of the Papyrus Club. My father showed it to me once."

"Do you have it?"

She shook her head. "But I think I know where it is."

He knew he shouldn't say it. As usual, it came out by itself: "Where would you suggest we look?"

"At his cottage."

Her white Volvo felt like a pair of mittens on a snowy day. It was warm and comfortable and, compared to Wolenski's Toyota, made him feel as safe as a baby in a motorized pram.

They drove across the river and then south till they came to an area he recognized. She passed through the campus and made a right onto a private access road that led to a small group of houses. At the bottom of the road she pulled over and stopped.

"His cottage is the one closest to the brook," she said, pointing to a pleasant one-story building with a rustic covering of fir.

They walked part way and then, when they got to a pebble path that led directly to the shingled cottage, they suddenly stopped.

The front door was sealed with tape. A sign on the door read, DO NOT ENTER—BY ORDER OF PORTLAND POLICE DEPARTMENT.

"You haven't been here since . . ." He glanced at her questioningly.

She looked pale and distraught as she shook her head.

"Would you like to go back to the car?"

She shook her head again. "I'll be all right," she said. Then, taking a deep breath, she walked to the door and began ripping off the tape.

It was an idyllic spot, he thought to himself, as he watched her unseal the door. There were trees and flowers. And there was the brook, no more than twenty feet away, which made cheery, gurgling sounds as it splashed over the polished rocks. In short, it was a splendid place for murder. But, then again, it wasn't his father.

He was mulling these thoughts over in his head, as she searched for the proper key to insert into the lock, when a wasp settled on his nose. He wasn't certain what it was at first.

"Listen," he said quietly, "I'm terribly allergic. Last time

94

one bit me on the arm it swelled up like a ripe banana. I can't even imagine what it would do to my schnozz!"

She took a hanky from her purse and with a flick she brushed it off. "They're always around here," she said, finally finding the right key from her assortment. "They live in a nest tucked into the cornice up there." She pointed to a brownish thing hanging from the gutter.

"You could probably spray them down with a hose," said Joseph, offering advice from his storehouse of personal experience.

"Not likely," said Abigail, pushing open the door, "My father studied them, you know . . ." Her voice trailed off as she suddenly saw the devastation that awaited her.

They didn't even need to walk inside to see that the front room had been demolished—curtains, window shades, bric-a-brac, shelving, books, records—everything had been heaped in a pile in the middle of the floor. All the furniture had been turned over, its lining had been ripped out and its insides gutted. Floorboards had been prised up. There were holes smashed into the plaster walls. The lath underneath the plaster had even been chiseled out. The electrical switch boxes had been removed. The knobs taken off the interior doors. The side panelling had been torn away from the heating elements attached to the baseboards. On the ceilings the light fixtures had been pulled down.

In fact, everything that could been done to the place short of running through it with a bulldozer, had already happened. It was a little like watching a vandalized corpse, Joseph thought.

He glanced over at her and saw the terrible look in her face. Then, he realized, she was staring at something. He followed her line of vision to the opposite wall and saw the huge ugly letters that covered it which read: KILL THE SPOTTED OWL!

"I'm sorry," he said, softly.

It was only then that she put her head on his shoulder and began to cry her heart out.

Chapter 13

She was too shaken to sit behind the steering wheel so Joseph drove her home. It took no more than twenty minutes to get back to her house. Even considering a stop they made for a quick drink to settle her nerves, they had been gone no more than an hour and a half.

He sensed there was something funny going on when he pulled the Volvo over to the curb and stopped. A tan Mercedes with its engine idling was parked opposite to them on the other side of the street. Its windows were tinted, so Joseph didn't have a clear view in, but he had the distinct impression that someone inside was observing them as he and Abigail got out.

On the other hand, he was sensitive to cars with tinted glass. He never trusted them or their owners. Especially if the car was a Mercedes.

"You feeling OK now?" he asked Abigail as they walked up to her house.

There was a little nod which he took to mean that she'd survive but wasn't quite over the shock yet.

"I'll use your phone to call a cab if you don't mind," he said, as she unlocked her door. "We'll keep in touch."

They went inside. Then he realized it wasn't over yet. They could do little more than stare. She probably was too emotionally drained to show much sign of distress—at least, that's what he thought. He, on the other hand, was flabbergasted.

The inside of the house, like the cottage, had been demolished. A professional wrecking crew couldn't have done a better job if they had been paid twice the going rate. The beautiful Scandinavian designs had been pounded into kindling. The impressionist prints were torn to shreds. The glass coffee table was smashed into tiny bits of silicon, the chrome legs bent. The stereo was little more than rubble. The house plants were dumped from their pots, the soil emptied onto the carpet. The white sofa he had sat on twice before was thrown upside down and all the stuffing was torn out.

In the hallway the tapestries had been torn from the wall. But the ultimate disaster was saved for the kitchen. And here Abigail put a delicate hand over her mouth and let out a little whimper.

The glass greenhouse dormer which had given so much charm to the kitchen had been smashed with such brutal force that the steel molding into which the glass was built now was twisted like the skeletal remains of an old church in Hiroshima.

She was standing, dumbly now, with a blank look on her face.

"Come on," he said. And grabbing her by the hand, he pulled her out.

They were sitting in a neighborhood café several blocks from the Overton place. It was empty except for them and the man behind the counter.

"You ought to call the police," said Joseph, sipping his coffee.

She shook her head. "I couldn't possibly deal with them. Not yet," she said.

"How about Henry? Shouldn't you contact him?"

"Henry?" She let a tiny smile appear on her face. "He's the last person I'd call!"

"Another friend perhaps? Isn't there someone who could help?"

She lifted her cup, more to warm her hands than drink. "I have friends who would help—help clean up the mess, that is. Hardly anyone who would understand." She looked at him. "How could they?"

He saw something in her eyes and realized that she was someone special. It was an instinctual thing. He might have been wrong—he had been wrong before. But he preferred to believe he was right.

"You can't just leave it like that," he said.

"No. Of course." She sipped at her drink.

"But you can't stay there either. Not by yourself."

"I wasn't planning to," she said. She looked into his eyes again. She appeared lost and defenseless. "I was going through an important change in my life. Even before my father . . ." She stopped.

He stared at her without saying anything. There was nothing to say.

She smiled, a little bitterly he thought. "Perhaps my house was destroyed before someone took an axe to it."

"Philosophy is fine, but you still have to do something," he said.

Her lips were pressed together in a look of defiance. "I have to find out what happened to my father!"

"Then what?"

"Then I'll find out what happened to myself."

He couldn't argue with that, even if he wanted to.

He convinced her to phone the police. She arranged to meet them at the café. He waited with her till they came.

"Where will you stay tonight?" he asked.

"I haven't decided yet," she replied.

He had probably made up his mind before he asked her. It wasn't a conscious thing. "Maybe I can help you," he said. "Maybe you can help me."

"I'd like that," she said.

He looked at his watch. "It's half-past two," he said. "I've got some things to take care of. I'd like you to check into a hotel—the Park Lane. Do you know it?"

"I know where it is," she said. "What should I do?"

"Just keep your eyes and ears open," he replied. "Especially on the third floor."

He stopped back at his own hotel to make a few calls.

When you need a drink, it's time to go back to the well, he told himself as he dialled the number.

Nickels set him up with someone else.

Sandra Stately was the reporter who had interviewed the widow of the lumberjack who was killed.

"She lives in Happy Valley," said Stately. "Has five kids and an unpaid mortgage."

"Would she be hard to see?"

"Probably not. But I'm not sure it would be worth your time. I spent an entire afternoon with her and didn't come back with a hell of a lot."

"She must have been pretty bitter," said Joseph.

"Not really," Stately replied. "I got the feeling she's the type who finds solace in her faith, no matter what goes wrong. One of her kids has leukemia. She's had to go on welfare. If she were bitter, she'd probably have gone insane." Stately stopped talking for a minute. Then she said, "Curious you're asking about her though . . ."

"Why's that?"

"I just spoke to her the other day. Things are beginning to look up. An insurance policy she never knew existed just paid off."

"So soon?" said Joseph. "Insurance companies I'm familiar with tend to be a little slower doling out their monies."

"And I bet the ones you know don't pay out in cash."

"You mean they paid her in cash?"

"Strange, isn't it? In fact, she said a young woman appeared at her door, from out of the blue, and handed her the money."

"I guess sometimes it just drops into your lap, huh? How about the rest of the community there? How did they respond to Russell's death?"

"A lot of them were very angry."

"Angry enough to take revenge?"

"On whom?"

"Professor Bright, maybe."

"These are pretty solid folks. A tight knit group. They might hate environmentalists, but I don't think they're ready to take up arms against them. I wouldn't want to pass out leaflets about protecting the spotted owl down there now. But I doubt if any lumbermen or their wives would come up here and kill a college professor in the middle of the night because he wants to clean dioxin from the river."

"Yeah," said Joseph. "I guess you're right."

He thanked her and hung up. And then he thought a bit.

Why would a lumberjack come and smash up Bright's house? To get revenge? That didn't make sense. No one accused Bright of spiking that tree. And, even so, what happened to his house went beyond revenge. It was methodical destruction. And, if he guessed right, made to look like it had been done by a psychopathic lumberjack.

If it was only Bright's house that had been pillaged, he might have had second thoughts. But why go on and smash up Abigail's? No, whoever did it was looking for something, all right. The question was what.

Joseph rubbed his aching jaw and thought of the connection. If he was to place a bet, he'd go with the missing link.

Katherine McCullough was known to have been with him a day or two before he was bumped off. They were close. Possibly closer than a student and teacher should be. She had access to certain information if only because of the people she knew. Now she was missing. It stood to reason that whatever Bright knew, she knew as well. And chances were she had given it to him.

Whatever Bright had hidden it was either found, ground up in the wrecking process or hidden so well that it would take more time than he had on earth (or at least in Portland) to find it. But the trail leading to Katherine (or Tara) was still warm. Anyway, it wasn't stone cold. The question was, how could he follow it?

He thought a moment and then, finding the card he had stashed in his wallet, he typed out Stavos' number on the buttons of the phone.

He recognized the gravelly voice of the woman who answered.

"Is Mr Stavos there?" asked Joseph, slightly disguising his speech.

"Who is this?" the woman asked.

It was a shot in the dark. But he hadn't any time to play

around. "I'm calling for Mr McCullough. There's some questions he needs to ask Mr Stavos concerning his daughter."

"That transaction no longer concerns us," she snapped. "If he has any questions, he should take it up with Mr Stavos' lawyer."

Sometimes he wished his brain worked faster. There were several responses he could make. But he didn't know which was the right one.

"We have," he said. "The problem is that Mr Stavos hasn't briefed his counsel properly. For example, the doctor you brought her to . . ."

"We only recommended Dr Phelps," she said, curtly. "You contacted him, not us!"

"Yes, of course," he said, quickly jotting the name down in his notebook. "I'll call you back." And he hung up.

He grabbed the *Yellow Pages* and let his fingers do the flying. "Doctors . . . doctors . . . doctors . . ." "See listing under Physicians" it said. He flipped through the pages to - "Physicians". The listings were all under specialties.

Cursing the phone company, he ruled out Osteopaths and Pediatricians and settled for Psychiatrists. He ran down the list of names. No Phelps.

He went through the entire list of physicians without any luck.

Radkin's rule number 27. When in doubt, dial for further information. In this case he called the Portland Branch of the Medical Association.

"I'm sorry," said the saccharine-voiced secretary who answered the phone, "I don't show a listing for a Dr Phelps. What's his specialty again?"

"Psychiatry—I think."

"Are you sure he's a medical doctor?"

"I don't think he's a witch doctor, if that's what you mean." On the other hand, he thought, maybe he is.

"No, I was thinking of a psychologist . . ."

"Possibly."

This time he went straight to the association.

"There's no Phelps on our active roles . . ." said the man who answered.

"How about inactive?" he said.

"Well, there was a Ronald Phelps."

Joseph licked the point of his pencil. "You got an address."

"He ran a clinic."

"Fine." His pencil was still poised. "I'll take it."

"However it was closed down."

His pencil drooped. "How come?"

"I couldn't say . . ."

"Listen," said Joseph, "I know you people stick close together. But if there's something fishy about this guy, I really need to know. It seems he reopened his clinic and I've got a friend who sent his daughter there . . ."

"Well, I really would suggest you tell your friend to reconsider," said the man.

"Could you give me a reason so I could tell my friend why?"

"Dr Phelps has been accused of some unorthodox practices."

"Can you spell that out?" Getting information from this guy was like trying to squeeze water from a day-old bagel, he thought.

"Quack therapy. Unlicensed drugs. Unregulated methods. A young man died while being treated in his clinic. His parents claim he was in good health. On the other hand, Dr Phelps also had his defenders."

"Could you give me the address of his clinic?"

"Can't you get it from your friend?"

"My friend's out of town. He left me in charge of his daughter."

"This is all very unusual," said the man as he read the address out.

He jotted down the address, hung up and then he placed another call.

"Hello," said the strangely modulated voice that answered. "I'm sorry that no one is here right now except me. If you wish you will have the opportunity to leave a message. But first— the survival of Bear Creek is threatened by people whose only interests are greed and squander. If you love the ancient forests and care about the survival of the species then you must be prepared to put your body on the line. The moment is fast approaching. Call back for further announcements. You may leave your message now. Beep."

"Hey, Wolenski, are you there?" asked Joseph, not sure whether Hal doubled as an answering machine or if Wolenski was just screening calls.

"Mr Radkin, I presume?"

"Right on the button. Ready for another chase?"

"Mr Wolenski is busy. He asks that you contact him later."

"Would you kindly tell Mr Wolenski that I need the services of his rat-trap car, now?"

"Mr Wolenski would like you to know that his car is not a rat trap. It is a fine automobile that is more reliable than the bus. Otherwise, he feels, you would not be calling him."

"Tell Mr Wolenski that he's absolutely correct—except for the fact that his rat-trap car is only better than a bus if you don't know where you're going. So tell him to please meet me at my hotel if he wishes to help me look for Tara!"

Chapter 14

The highway toward Boring was flat and dull, passing through the outskirts of eastern Portland without even a chuckle. He wondered why anyone would stick a town with a name like that. Maybe there wasn't any answer. Or maybe the question answered itself.

It took no more than a half hour to reach the countryside where the hidden grandeur of the region came into view. Looming before them, though still some miles away, was the rugged snow-capped peak of Mount Hood, shimmering in the atmosphere like a monumental dish of ice cream for the gods. To the south stretched the lowlands, feeding into the Willamette River, laced with small truck farms and groves of evergreens.

Following the road signs to Boring, they made a right onto a small, two-lane road. A mile further they began paralleling a rushing stream and, soon, coming to an old beam bridge, they crossed over.

The land on the other side was woody and green. It smelled of pine and wet mulch. They continued on five minutes more until they came to a crossroads. In the center triangle was a small building that served as a combination service station and general store.

Wolenski pulled up to the pump that was located by the side. He got out and stretched his skinny arms. Joseph slid himself over and got out too.

An elderly man dressed in denims and wearing a baseball cap came up and inspected them. He didn't seem to be in any hurry.

"You guys want somethin'?" he asked.

"Gas," said Joseph.

"Sure you don't want a tow truck?" The old man looked disparagingly at the beat-up car.

"You only serve Cadillacs?" asked Joseph, raising an eyebrow.

The old guy shrugged and moved himself painfully over to the pump. "How much you want?" he asked.

Joseph looked over at Wolenski who raised the fingers of one hand in the air.

"Five dollars," said Joseph.

"Sure you don't want me to fill it up—long as it's runnin' . . ."

"Five bucks," Joseph repeated. Then, pulling out his notebook and opening it up, he said, "You know a place called Shady Glen?"

The old guy didn't answer. He kept his wrinkled hand on the handle of the pump and watched the gauge cranking out the numbers.

Joseph repeated his question, thinking the old guy maybe was a little deaf.

"I heard you the first time," he said.

"So, do you know it?"

The old guy stopped the pump and withdrew the hose. He hung it back in its cradle and said, "I might."

"Which fork do we take? Right or left?"

"Either one. Don't really make much difference," said the old guy sticking out his hand. "Five bucks."

Joseph took out a five and handed it to the man. Then he handed him a single. "Nice business you got going here," he said.

The old guy took the single, folded it and put it in his pocket. "As I said, don't matter much. If you take the left fork, you turn right in about a mile. If you take the right fork you turn left."

They took the left fork and travelled on passing orchards and strawberry fields until they came to a dirt road with a handmade sign indicating the way to Shady Glen.

A few hundred feet of muddy pot holes led them to a group of small, white-washed cabins set back from the road and built into a grove of pines. As they turned into the gravel drive, a barking dog came up to greet them. Unlike Stavos' dobermans, however, this one seemed to be a friendly collie.

But there was no one else. For all appearances, the place seemed to be deserted.

They sat in the station wagon a while contemplating the scene. Except for the yapping dog and the sound of a curtain from an open window flapping in the breeze, it was quite silent.

Another wild goose chase, Joseph thought. Just a lousy waste of time.

Wolenski had gotten out and was walking toward one of the cottages as Joseph searched through his pockets for a cigarette butt to light. It was too far to have come on too little information, he thought. He felt angry at himself.

He found a crumpled butt and smoothed it out. He struck a light. The smoke had a brief narcotic effect which was all right.

Through the open window of a nearby cabin facing an old oak tree, he saw Wolenski's figure. It bent, then lowered, then disappeared.

Joseph climbed out of the station wagon and walked over to the cabin by the oak. The door was open. He walked inside.

Someone had been living here all right. But either they were lousy housekeepers or had vanished in the middle of the night. There was a single mussed-up bed, a small dresser with its empty drawers hastily pulled out, a wooden table on which rested a plate holding the remains of a fried egg, some stained utensils and a paper napkin that had been crushed and dropped into the plate. A straight back chair was knocked over on the floor as if someone had bumped into it in mid-flight.

Standing by the table, Joseph stuck his cigarette butt into the half-eaten egg yolk and estimated from its texture that it hadn't been sitting there for more than a day—two at most.

He didn't see him at first. Then he noticed his scrawny figure kneeling by the corner of the far wall. Joseph called to him. Wolenski didn't move.

Walking over to where he was kneeling on the floor, Joseph bent down too. Wolenski had been staring at something written on the wall. Whoever wrote it must have been sitting or lying in a contorted way in order to have written in that position.

It was done in soft, shaky lines, as if the writer had difficulty holding on to the pencil. It read: "The power of nothing has filled this emptiness of fear. Death will be the victor."

Wolenski turned and Joseph saw his face. It wore an expression of deep and immense sorrow.

They drove back the way they came. Past the strawberry fields and orchards till they came to the crossroads. He told Wolenski to pull into the parking bay of the service station they had been to before.

The old guy in the baseball cap was sitting on a folding chair by the air pump. Wolenski drove up to where he was seated and stopped.

Joseph rolled down his window. "How about some air?" he asked the old man.

"Air's for customers," the man said.

"We were here about ten minutes ago," said Joseph.

"I remember," said the old man.

"So we're customers."

"You were then. You shoulda gotten air then."

Joseph took a dollar out of his wallet and held it through the open window. "That place we went to—Shady Glen. Run by guy named Phelps, I understand."

The old guy took the dollar. "Used to be," he said.

"Used to be?" Joseph gave him a questioning look. "Not any more?"

"Need more air?" asked the man.

Joseph took out another dollar.

"Put on the market about six months ago," said the man, taking the dollar.

"You know who bought it?"

The man rubbed his chin.

Joseph handed him a dollar.

"Nope," said the man.

"See anyone staying there lately?"

The old guy stuffed the bills into his shirt pocket.

"Seen a light now and then from one of the cottages. Ain't

seen no one. Been pretty quiet. One of them fancy German cars come up there on occasion. Stayed for a while. Not long."

Joseph turned to Wolenski. "You want any more air?" he asked.

Wolenski shook his head, started the Toyota and drove off.

Twenty-five minutes later they were in downtown Portland.

Wolenski dropped him at the Cambridge Arms. Joseph stopped at the registration desk for his key and his messages and went up to his room. He looked through the slips of paper the desk clerk had handed him and then, taking off his jacket and shirt, went to the bathroom and washed up. Afterward, feeling somewhat refreshed, he took his materials to the writing table and went over them again, making some notes on hotel stationery he found in the drawer.

After he finished, he looked at the diagrams and doodles and lines and swatches and thought that what he had wasn't really much.

He called the Park Lane, as one of the messages requested.

"Abigail Bright," he told the operator when he was connected. "She's in room 508."

She answered on the first ring.

"How you feeling?" he asked.

"Better," she replied. "I'm glad you called. I'm getting restless here. I need to be doing something or I'll go nuts!"

"All right," he said, "I'll be over soon. Meet you in the downstairs bar."

She was sitting at a table nursing a glass of sherry when he came in. She was wearing a knitted suit of muted color that fit her nicely and was pleasant to the look.

He joined her and decided on a salad and to skip the alcohol in an uncharacteristic attempt to keep a clear head.

"What do you know about your father's relations with a young woman named Katherine McCullough?" he asked after placing his order.

She looked a little dismayed.

"We haven't much time, Abby," he said. "We've got to cut through the bullcrap fast."

"He was close to some of his students," she said. "Perhaps too close. I don't know if there was anything sexual . . ."

"I'm not here to pass moral judgement on anyone," he said. "Frankly, I don't care. She was old enough to make her own decisions . . ."

"And he was old enough to know better," she replied, with a slightly bitter air.

"Whatever. Katherine most likely was the one who gave your father whatever it was that got him in a jam. And it got her in one, too. She's missing. Might be in pretty bad shape."

"What happened to her?" she asked, looking even more dismayed.

"Your guess is as good as mine," he said. "I spoke to her dad yesterday. Not my favorite of people. He doesn't make any bones about his feelings—which aren't sugar coated. But family means a lot to him, if you get my drift."

She may have gotten his drift or maybe not. He couldn't tell. Her eyes seemed to be focused on something else.

"Do you see that man?" she suddenly asked, in a hushed voice, putting her manicured hand on his.

He turned around and looked.

"The man with the white moustache standing by the elevator. He's holding a newspaper . . ."

"What about him?" he asked.

"That's Felix Tobias—one of the chief honchos from Millennium Investments."

He glanced back at her. "How do you know?"

"You told me to keep my eyes open," she said. "And I did."

The elevator door opened and the man with the white moustache went in. Joseph grabbed Abigail by the hand and pulled her up.

"Hold the elevator please!" he called out.

They dashed through the central lobby and into the waiting lift.

The man with the white moustache let go of the door. "They come every fifteen seconds, you know," he said in a tone of annoyance.

Joseph smiled, apologetically and pointed up. "Left my wallet. Silly. Wouldn't want to leave it all alone too long."

"I know what you mean," said the man, opening his newspaper.

It was the *Wall Street Journal*. Joseph noticed he had opened it to the stock report page.

"You play the market?" Joseph asked.

The man grunted.

"Any tips?"

The elevator stopped at the third floor. The man folded his journal again and glanced at Abigail. He seemed to like what he saw. "Keep your eye on paper," he said as he walked out.

The door started to close. Joseph moved his foot to hold it open. "Isn't this our floor?" he asked Abigail, giving her a wink.

"I think it is," she said.

They were getting off when a man in a dark suit stepped up to them and said, "Sorry. This is a restricted area. Could I see your key?"

"What floor is this?" asked Joseph.

"Three."

"I guess we got off too soon," he said.

The man waited at their side till the elevator came again. They got in, the door shut and they went up to the fifth.

"What do you think that's all about?" she asked, when they reached the floor her room was on.

"I don't know," said Joseph. He wondered that himself.

They walked to 508 and she let him in.

He poured himself a drink of water and then began pacing back and forth from one end of the tiny room to the other while she sat on the bed and watched him.

Finally he said, "There's something fishy going on."

"All that pacing up and down and that's what you come up with?" She almost laughed.

He looked at her as if she were intruding on some delicate mental gymnastics. "What did you say?"

She shook her head. "Never mind."

"We have to get onto that floor," he said, starting to pace back and forth again.

"To do what?"

Stopping abruptly, he stared at her, amazed that she hadn't

followed his train of thought. "To find out what's going on down there!"

"Why?"

"Because someone wants me to—for reasons I don't quite understand yet."

"Is that any reason to do it?" she asked, looking at him somewhat astounded.

"In my line of work, yes."

"You have a plan, I take it?"

"Not exactly," he admitted. "But something will come."

She nodded. "I see."

"Wait here," said Joseph. "Ten minutes. Fifteen at the most."

"You'll be back?" she asked.

"I sincerely hope so," he said.

Chapter 15

He took the service stairs down as far as they could go. A door at the bottom said "Hotel Staff Only". He let himself in.

There was a long narrow hallway. He walked quickly, trying to think of a good story in case he was stopped. He could think of lots of stories but he wasn't sure any of them were good.

Radkin's rule number 22. Always look confident even if you haven't the foggiest notion what you're going to do next.

He could hear the sounds of activity ahead as the hall turned abruptly to the right. It grew louder. He passed one door and then another. Then the direction of the hallway shifted left.

Straight ahead was the kitchen. Lunch must have still been going on as there was a flurry of activity. Waiters were bursting in and out of the swinging doors like half-crazed wind-up penguins. He figured the food was the same as the image in his head—fast and fishy.

He continued on. Back straight. Eyes focused ahead.

"Excuse me."

He felt his stomach ache. He turned, expecting to see the house dick glower.

Instead, a young man with a lock of damp hair falling over his face looked at him questioningly. "Could you tell me where I can find some extra forks? One of the dishwasher's broken. The other one is in the middle of its cycle and I can't wait!"

"Why don't you try washing some out by hand?" Joseph suggested.

"I thought we weren't allowed to do that."

Joseph winked. "One time. Who's to know?"

The guy pushed back his hair and grinned. "Yeah! Thanks!"

"Hey! Wait a second!" Joseph called after him.

The guy turned around. His hair had fallen over his eyes again.

"Where the hell do they put the uniforms?" he asked. "I'm supposed to check the sizes."

"Uniform room," he pointed. "Straight down the hall. Second left."

Lucky break, he thought as he walked on. Sometimes it breaks right. Sometimes it breaks wrong.

He saw the sign. He opened the door.

It broke wrong.

A woman sat behind a counter. She was knitting.

Think fast! he told himself. Think fast!

She looked up at him. Her eyebrows raised.

"Laundry?" she asked.

He nodded.

She pointed with her knitting needle. There was a huge plastic bag. He picked it up. He opened the door.

"Hey, mister!"

He turned. She looked at him and raised an eyebrow. She pointed with her needle. There was another one.

He picked up the other bag and tried to balance it in his arms with the first. The two bags together were almost as big as him.

Struggling out the door, he waddled on down the hallway. There must have been a hundred pounds of laundry he thought. Maybe even more. And, as he made the turn and headed toward the exit door, he wondered whether he could qualify in the *Guinness Book of Records* for a combination of the world's stupidest heist and slowest getaway.

He thought of that as he struggled up five flights of stairs. That was the way his mind worked. Long ago he had decided that given the choice, he'd rather laugh than cry. But the way his arms ached, crying was definitely on the agenda.

He kicked at the door of 508 several times before she answered. She didn't see him at first behind the two giant bags of laundry.

"What the bloody hell kept you?" he cursed as he pushed his way in, "My arms are about to fall off!"

113

She watched, a little amused and slightly horrified, as he dumped the dirty laundry on her bed. The heap was so high that the clothes began dropping to the floor.

"Where did you get all this?" Her hands were on her hips.

He shrugged. "Some guy sold 'em to me cheap. Said they were mink coats." He looked down at the uniforms. "I guess I was taken."

Abigail started sifting through the clothes. "They're in pretty bad shape," she said.

"So we're sloppy." He pulled out an outfit and held it in front of him. "How does this look?"

"Awful!" she said, holding her nose.

He pulled out a maid's costume and tossed it to her. "Try this on," he suggested.

"They wear them so short!" she said, putting it in front of her and turning to the mirror. She looked back at him. He wiggled his eyebrows.

"It doesn't matter," he said. "We're just on a search and seizure mission. We should be out of there before they get a chance to see the crease marks."

She took the maid's outfit into the bathroom as he pulled off his trousers and put on a room service uniform.

"What are we seizing?" she asked through the door.

"We don't know," he replied, trying on a jacket which didn't fit. He pulled it off and grabbed another one. "We need to search first."

She came out in her tight-fitting maid's costume. He hadn't realized before how bosomy she was. "I guess I like to plan things out a little more."

"You would," he said. "You're a lawyer."

"Who might end up in jail."

"So you probably know all the judges anyway," he said, buttoning his jacket and slicking down his hair.

"That's the problem," said Abigail. She looked at him and shook her head. "We'll have to do something about your face."

"Sorry," he replied. "It's the only one I got."

"I mean the bruises."

"Got any suggestions?" he asked.

She took out her makeup kit and did him up.

*

They stuffed the extra uniforms in a broom closet down the hall, hiding the key to her room in there as well so that whoever got back first would have access to it. Then they headed for the stairs.

"It might be all right for you to wander around ad-libbing life," she said as they walked down to the third level. "But I don't work that way. I need something more thought out."

"Don't worry about it," he replied. "Just see if you can get into some rooms. Say you're checking the linen—anything. Snoop around. They've closed that floor off, for heaven's sake. Something's got to be going on."

Abigail gave him a curious look. Then she asked, "You do things like this often?"

"Occasionally," he said.

He pushed open the fire door a crack and peeked into the third floor hall. Turning back to her he said, "Nuts. They've got someone guarding every blasted entrance."

"So what do we do?" she asked.

He rubbed his chin. "Tactical retreat. Get ammunition. Then brazen it out." He pointed. "Back up to the fifth floor."

"This is getting tiring," she said as they trudged back up again.

"Think how I feel!" he responded. "Lugging all that fucking laundry up here!"

"You could have just dumped it someplace and brought up a few."

"And how would you have felt in an outfit a size smaller than the one you have on?"

She looked down at her cramped chest. "Not very well."

He nodded.

They had reached the fifth floor again.

"I remembered there were some leftovers from room service in the hall," he said, pointing to a tray.

He began to combine the fluid from the glasses and then fixed up several plates with the leftovers. He picked up the tray. "How do I look?" he asked.

"Like the angel of death," she replied. "What do I take?"

He motioned his head toward the linen closet. "Just grab anything in there. It doesn't matter what."

She opened the door and took a look. She came out with a toilet bowl plunger and a brush.

"Great," he said. "All those guys are probably constipated. They'll consider it an omen if you wave that plunger at them."

They walked over to the elevator.

"Who goes first?" she asked.

They flipped a coin. She won.

"Bye, bye,' she waved the plunger as he got on the elevator and pushed the button.

He held the tray level to his face as he got off the elevator on the third floor, hoping that the man in the dark suit stationed there wouldn't recognize him.

The guard took only a brief glance and then looked down again at the book he was reading.

Joseph walked quickly down the hall and wondered what kind of book a guy like that would read. *Twenty-One Ways to Skin An Intruder*? Who knows, he thought. Maybe he's reading Gerassi's great new opus on the life of Sartre. You can never tell.

He headed for the room number that had been written on the card. It was as good a one as any.

He knocked and then walked in. Brazen is as brazen does, he thought.

It was a large suite with enough electronic gear to radiate the city. Computers, ticker tapes, modems, fax. A giant TV screen was tuned to the New York stock exchange—or maybe London or Tokyo. They probably looked the same, he thought.

Some high flyers were seated round a table and looked up as he came in.

"Room service!" He smiled at them politely.

He saw Tobias, the man with the white moustache, look at him suspiciously. Tobias didn't recognize him, of course. Joseph knew that. Those guys just see a uniform, he told himself.

"Anybody call room service?" asked Tobias.

"Maybe Headly," someone said.

"Where's Headly?"

"In the john," said someone.

"Just leave it," Tobias said, looking at Joseph again.

Joseph glanced around the room once more hoping something would strike his eye while he slowly put the stuff from the tray onto a sidetable.

A lean young man in a silk suit and well conditioned hair that would have looked at home on an Australian beach went over to him and stuffed a five spot that stank of cologne into his pocket.

The silk suit smiled condescendingly. "OK, kid, you can go."

Joseph thought he could divide his age in half and still be older than that jerk. He smiled, affably anyway. In fact he displayed all his teeth—those that remained.

"Can I be of further service, sir?"

"Why don't you collect those empties and take 'em with you," said Tobias, waving his hand at a scattering of bottles and glasses.

Good for you, sir, he wanted to say. Very good for you.

They were talking business stuff as he cleaned up. Like bonds and interest rates. They kept punching things up on the computer.

"How long till blast off?" someone said.

"Keep your shirt on. We still have some time left," said Tobias. "Anyone heard from San Francisco?"

"Nothing yet," said the silk suit.

"Well get him on the friggin phone!" shouted Tobias. "We need those goddamn photos!" He turned to Joseph. "Aren't you finished yet?"

"Just about . . ."

At that moment the door burst open and a man with a loose tie dangling from his neck breezed in. "We've reached agreement with Morgan Trust!" he said.

The room was suddenly charged with electricity.

Tobias punched the air. "Ok! We're ready to roll!" He pointed to Joseph. "Someone get this guy out of here!"

He had been waiting about twenty minutes and was just about to call the cops (what he'd say was optional) when she finally came into the room still holding the plunger and the brush.

Her hair was matted to her perspiring face. Her uniform was a mess. In fact she looked a little like a mouse that had just crawled up from the sewers.

"What the hell happened to you?" he asked.

She dropped the plunger and brush onto the floor and she fell into a chair. "I knocked on one of the doors. There were two men. They were very glad to see me . . ."

He wasn't sure he wanted to hear the rest. "They didn't . . ."

"They did. Many times. And it still didn't flush."

"I don't get it," he said.

She looked at him wearily. "Their toilet. It really was stuffed up."

He laughed. "Say—maybe you'll go down in the annals of espionage as 'The Great Toilet Spy'!"

Grimacing at him, she reached into her bodice and pulled out some folded sheets of paper. She held them out. "Alright, Mr 007. Ante-up."

"Mine? I got it all in here." He pointed to his head. Then, taking the papers from her, he shuffled through.

"I found them in the trash can when I was cleaning up," she said. "They were the only things that seemed of the slightest interest."

It was mostly financial gibberish, meaningless to the untutored eye. Except for one. It was another copy of the local shipping report—the same one that had been sent to him at his hotel. Only on this copy, one of the arrivals was circled: a ship which sailed under the name *São Paulo* and was bound for Rio.

"Does it mean anything to you?" she asked.

He studied the clipping and then shook his head. "No. But let's find out a little more about it."

Picking up the phone he placed a call to Nickels.

"You know," Nickels said when he got on the line, "I do work sometimes."

"Sure," said Joseph, "we all do. Just connect me with

someone who keeps track of the comings and goings at the port."

"That'll be Jack Parkins," said Nickels. "I'll put you through."

Parkins didn't know a thing about the *São Paulo*. "But I'll tell you this," he said. "It's docked at pier twenty-one. And it's pretty strange to have a ship from South America that far up the river."

"Why?" asked Joseph.

"She's almost at the falls," he said. "No commerce up there except paper and lumber. And you wouldn't send either of them to Brazil."

"Maybe she's unloading then," said Joseph.

"What?" asked Parkins. "The warehouses are all downstream from there. No, the ships using that berthing space mostly pick up paper cylinders for customers overseas."

"So why not Brazil?"

"They manufacture more newsprint then we do for half the cost. Of course, just because it's a Brazilian ship and lists Rio as its next port of call doesn't mean it couldn't be taking cargo someplace else."

"How about if it were contraband?" asked Joseph.

"Like drugs? I doubt it. That kind of stuff is offloaded at sea. I'd say that it's probably picking up finished paper and bringing it to another port of call that isn't listed."

"Thanks for your help," said Joseph, hanging up.

She looked at him. "Dead end?"

"Maybe," he replied. He thought a moment and then he asked "Isn't McCullough Paper located at the falls?"

"Yes. Close by."

"The research plant is there as well?"

"That's right."

"Come on," he said, getting up quickly.

"Where are we going?" she asked.

"For a ride." He headed to the door.

"Wait a second!" she called after him.

He turned around.

"I can't go like this." She motioned to the maid's uniform she was wearing.

"Why not?" he asked. "You think I only go out with lawyers?"

His humor was lost on her. She gave him a serious look and said, "I think we better change our gear."

Chapter 16

Willamette City was an old mill town. Of course in Oregon terms, "old" was just a mite over one century. It lay about ten miles south of Dunthorp, where McCullough had his home.

A dirty concrete bridge straddled the river and took you straight into the center of the smoke-filled town and about two blocks from the mill. You didn't see it at first—the mill, that is—but you knew it was there from the odor.

Most of the housing was situated on the bluff that overlooked the town center. From the cliffs you had a great view of the river as it plunged over the mighty falls.

You got to the bluff by either driving up a winding road that rose steeply from the embankment or by means of an old municipal elevator that was built into the side of the hill just a stone's throw from Wanda's Café.

That was where the grey-haired woman with the tattoo of a sailor on her right arm told Joseph to go if he wanted to know anything about what was happening around town. Since she ran the municipal elevator, Joseph felt confident that her information was at least as reliable as a taxi driver's.

Wanda's was just about empty when they came in.

"6.00 a.m., you couldn't find a seat in here," said the hefty waitress, dressed in a blue uniform that probably was starched and ironed when she started that morning but fit her now like a smock she had pulled from Joseph's dirty clothes bag. "In an hour the mill changes shifts, so we'll be packed again. In between we only got our regulars like Ben," she pointed to an old codger sitting at a table on the other side of the café, "and a few tourists that Ida sends us."

"She the one who runs the elevator?" asked Joseph.

"She's the one. Been there twenty years—ever since she left the service. Maybe more." The waitress licked the tip of her pencil. "What'll you folks have?"

Joseph ordered a stack of hot cakes, the house specialty he was told. Abigail just had some toast. "And ask Ben if he'd like to join us for some coffee," Joseph told the waitress.

"That'll be a first," she replied. "'Course he'd love it. All he ever does is talk."

She went to fill the order and on her way whispered something in the old guy's ear. In a while the codger came over to their table and sat down.

"You folks from around here?" he asked rubbing the grizzle on his chin and trying to make out whether he knew either of them or if his mind was playing tricks on him again.

"Depends on what you mean by 'around'," said Joseph. "Portland's twenty miles."

"Twenty miles, you're in a different world," said the codger. "When I came here this place was still mostly forest. The best way to get here from Portland was by boat. They'd just completed the locks at that time. 'Course it was just for small river boats. Any ship of consequence had to dock downstream from the falls."

"How long has the mill been around?" asked Joseph.

"Long as the town," the codger replied. The waitress came and poured them out some coffee. He lifted his cup. "Thanks for the java," he said. "'Course it was a saw mill first," he continued. "Paper didn't come till later."

"I'm sure you've seen lots of changes since you've been here," said Abigail.

"Yes and no," said the codger. "The town ain't changed too much since the war—the second one I'm talkin' about, not them little conflicts they had since. Up till then the town was changin' every day. Even was the time they thought this was gonna be the capital of the state."

"How about recently?" asked Joseph.

"Recently?" The codger ran his wrinkled fingers through brittle hair. "Recently, I've been gettin' old."

Abigail smiled gently. "Seems to me your eyes are still clear."

"I see things, OK," he said. "Some things younger folks

don't—or maybe they don't want to." He shook his head. "I couldn't say whether I see 'em clear or not anymore."

"There's talk about some big changes coming soon," said Joseph. "Lots of money floating around."

The old codger squinted his eyes. "You two ain't your ordinary tourists."

"I'm a journalist," Joseph admitted. "I'm doing a story on the new pulp mill. I understand they set up a prototype of the plant to test out a new bleaching system."

"That's what they say." The codger looked a little dubious.

"Actually, you can see it from the bluffs," said Abigail. "We went up there on the elevator before coming here."

"I know it's there," said the codger. "What they're doin' inside is another matter, ain't it?"

Joseph looked at the old guy and tried to decide what to make of him. "I'm not sure I understand," he said.

"Well I never seen a pulp mill run like a secret military plant till now. They got such high security, ain't nobody gettin' near there. All the workers they use come from out of town. And there ain't too many of them, from what I can make out. They come and go. Never talk to no one."

"The paper industry is getting highly competitive," Abigail explained. "It's not all that unusual to have private research and development under tight security. Especially with so much money at stake . . ."

"Sure," he said. "You're right, I guess. After all, what do I know? Then, of course, there's that ship sitting out there for the last week. Bringin' stuff in to that little blockhouse in the middle of the river—just in the dead of the night, of course. Between shifts when no one's around. Don't make much sense. But what the hell do I know?"

"What do you think is going on?" asked Joseph, taking out his notebook and jotting down some notes.

"Don't rightly know," said the old man.

"If you had to guess," said Abigail.

"What comes from down south?" he asked back.

"Lots of things," said Joseph.

"Lots of things don't make people rich. Just some things does."

"What have you seen?" asked Abigail.

"Not much," he replied. "Just what looked like logs. But appearances can be deceiving."

"Anything else?" asked Joseph.

"Some strange-lookin' people nosin' around."

Joseph narrowed his eyes. "What did they look like?"

The codger smiled. There was a wide gap in his mouth where some teeth had rotted out. "Not too different from yourself," he said. "Maybe a little older. Not as much hair and a little heftier maybe. Seen 'em out on the cliff takin' photographs."

"Lots of tourists must do that," said Abigail.

"Not too many tourists take their pictures at night," he replied. "Just standin' out there on the cliff alone, without a flash or nothin'."

Joseph took out his card, wrote a number on the back and handed it to the old man. "Give me a call if you see anything else, all right?"

"Sure," the codger said, staring at the card for a while before putting it in his pocket. "And thanks for the java."

After leaving Wanda's they took a ride up to the top of the bluffs. They pulled over at an isolated lookout point to observe the view.

It was a magnificent panorama. To the south-east and jutting behind them were the mountains and the forest. From there, the river cut through the canyons like a hungry snake. Right before it reached the town it suddenly widened into a delta. A few hundred yards further, it swept over the gigantic falls in a mighty torrent.

The paper mill was spread over a large piece of land which jutted out into the massive lake that formed on the other side of the falls. About fifty yards closer was a small island which contained the blockhouse where the research plant was.

Abigail brought out a pair of binoculars from her glove compartment. "Bird watcher," she explained.

He took them from her hand. "Let's see if we can find us a canary."

They were powerful enough for them to get close up. He could see the hubbub surrounding the mill. On one end the wood chips and sawdust were piled in mountainous heaps. Along the side were barrels of chemicals stacked near open conveyors. At the other end was a massive storage area where the finished paper was kept. He could see the trucks loading up with pallets.

Then, running his magnified sight to the nearside of the river, he saw the blockhouse, in contrast deadly quiet. Surrounded by a high barbed-wire fence, only the white smoke pouring from a chimney gave a clue that anything was going on within.

"You can't see the loading dock for the research station from here. I think you'd have to get right down to the falls in order to view what was going on."

He handed her the glasses and adjusted her line of sight by turning her head gently with his hands. "That's the ship," he said. "It's berthed over by the bend in the river. I didn't see any deck cargo."

"There doesn't seem to be any activity at all," she said. "No loading or unloading. Nothing at all."

"She's probably been unloaded already. According to the shipping report we saw, she's been there a few days now." Joseph took back the glasses and focused in. "And she's floating way above her high water marks. She's pretty empty now."

"Or else her cargo doesn't weigh very much," said Abigail.

Joseph gave her back the glasses. "It just doesn't make sense," he said.

"What doesn't?"

"The drug thing—if that's what the old guy was implying. I mean, why? It's not like there's any shortage of the stuff coming into the States. There are plenty of private airstrips were they can bring in cocaine. And ships are usually offloaded in the open seas, transferring stuff to smaller boats that anchor in a thousand different coves. And even if they were unloading drugs, why would they bring them to a pulp mill research plant? Why not just hide them in the woods?"

"Why no local employment in the research plant?" she asked him back.

"You answered that yourself when you said that research is big bucks—especially if you're breaking into new technology."

"It still seems vaguely suspicious," she replied, looking at him curiously.

He had turned away. His attention had been drawn by something else. "That car," he said, pointing to a tan Mercedes that was slowly driving toward them from the top of the hill. "Isn't that the same one we saw by your place?"

"It could have been . . ." she started to say.

He grabbed her hand and pulled. "I don't like the looks of this," he said, moving over toward her Volvo. He opened the driver's door and motioned for her to get in. "Let me drive, OK?"

She didn't object. He jumped in beside her. The key was still in the ignition. He quickly started the engine.

The Mercedes had pulled in behind them. The front window was rolled down. Through the rear-view mirror, Joseph could see what looked like the silver flash of metal.

Shoving the gearshift into first, he lurched forward, leaving behind the smell of burning rubber. The Mercedes leapt out after them.

He threw the Volvo into second, grinding the gears. He picked up speed, but not enough.

The Mercedes, faster, leaner, sped around the side till they were neck and neck.

"Get your head down!" he shouted.

She doubled up and buried herself in the seat just as the sound of shattering glass blasted around them. He felt a prickly sensation on the side of his face like the point of a red hot poker as he forced the gears back into first and gripped the slippery wheel with everything he had left—spinning it as far as it would go while braking and then stomping his foot down on the gas.

The Volvo whipped around one hundred and eighty degrees, sliding laterally onto the pebble siding. One rear wheel spun precariously over the side of the cliff while the other shot pebbles behind it like shrapnel. Then, suddenly, they lurched forward again.

He raced up the hill and then screeched left onto a road that led to the upper side of town. Swerving into the first service station he saw, he slammed on the brakes and skidded to a halt.

Across the street was the police station.

He looked at her. She looked at him. She was speechless. But he was too.

It was a couple of minutes before either of them could talk.

"Have you ever done that before?" she finally asked.

He shook his head. "No. Have you?"

"Not in this life."

Her face was so white that he could have believed she already left this life and had gone on to the next.

She was staring at him. "Your face!" she said.

"There's really nothing I can do about it. You already made it up." He shrugged.

Placing her fingers on his cheek, she slid them downwards and then displayed the tips to him. They were full of blood.

"The side of your face caught some particles of glass." She opened her purse and got out a handkerchief. "Use this for the time being," she said, "it's clean."

Her hand was trembling slightly as she gave it to him.

He took the cloth and pressed it against his cheek. It was only then that he felt the pain.

"I'm frightened," she said. She uttered it without a great deal of emotion. It was just stating a simple fact.

"I'm not too elated right now myself," he replied. The plasma had soaked its way through the handkerchief and was now oozing through his hand.

"Look at yourself!" she said. "You're dripping with blood!"

He saw himself in the window glass. And at the same time he realized something else. There were others looking in. In fact, he was suddenly aware that the car was surrounded by people, gawking, staring, hands in pockets or finger on chin, quietly observing them like vultures or blood-thirsty vampires from the city of the dead.

Chapter 17

The surgeon at the county police station cleaned him up and said he'd live.

The cop they talked to was a little doubtful. He seemed to be more curious about Joseph's reason for being there than wanting to find out who tried to bump them off.

"You sure it was a gun and not a rock?" asked the cop. His feet were propped up on his desk. He was chewing on a little twig.

"Did you find a rock in the car?" asked Joseph.

"No. But we didn't find no bullet neither."

"That's because the window on the driver's side was open. It continued out!"

"So could've the rock." The cop smiled patiently, like he had heard it all before. "You certain you saw a gun?"

"Yes."

"Through the rear-view mirror from a hundred feet away? Sure it weren't a piece of metal jewelry stickin' out?"

"I'm sure."

Abigail piped up. "He pointed it into my face, for goodness sakes!"

"What did this feller look like, Ma'am." The cop straightened up in his chair. He was tall and lanky and, from his weathered face, appeared to have been around for a while.

She hesitated. "I couldn't say. It all happened so fast."

The cop nodded. "I see."

"No you don't!" She said angrily.

He turned back to Joseph. "The problem is that there's been some people comin' in, stirrin' up a bit of trouble lately. City folk, mostly, who seem to like trees an awful lot. Like trees more than people, some would say. They look down at the river over there and see a log or two floating around, cut down by the few lumbermen who still got their jobs, and they get a little excited. Start tryin' to find a judge to issue an injunction. They never stop to think that for every injunction there's another man put out of work, another mortgage left unpaid, another family evicted from their home. Every once in a while one of the boys hears stories like this and kinda over reacts a little . . ."

Joseph raised his eyebrows. "I'd call that more than a little over reaction, wouldn't you?"

The cop took a newspaper from the side of his desk and handed it to Joseph. "This belong to you?" he asked. "We found it on the seat of your car."

It was the copy of the *Midnight Special* Wolenski had given him.

"Must have fallen out of my pocket," Joseph said.

"Kinda strong for these parts," said the cop, looking at him less than kindly.

"Someone gave it to me," said Joseph, a little defensively. "Anyway, whoever shot at us—and someone did shoot at us!—didn't shoot at us for that!"

"Well, I'll grant you this. Whoever broke your window didn't like you much," the cop said. And then he walked out, leaving his clerk to fill out the police report.

Except for the window and a couple of bald spots on the tires, the Volvo was still in good repair. Drivable, anyway.

"It's not that I don't trust you," said Abigail. "But maybe you should give me back the keys."

He did and she drove.

They were half-way to Portland when he looked at her and said, "That club you mentioned your father was in—at Stanford . . ."

"The Papyrus Club."

"Yes. It would have been good if we'd found that group picture."

"I've been thinking about that," she said. "There was a box

of photographs my father gave me after my mother died. Maybe it's there."

"Do you think you could try to find it?"

"You mean go back to my place? Now?" The muscles in her face tightened.

"I know it's a lot to ask," he said. "But I think it's important."

"What about you?"

"Drop me off at the central library," he said. "There's something I want to look up." He glanced at his watch. "It's three o'clock now. I'll call your hotel in a couple of hours."

The library was crowded. Not with students, but with the new habitués, the urban homeless, who used the place as a refuge from the rain. They brought with them whatever fit into a plastic sack which they kept close to their chair, fearful, perhaps, that even such meager possessions might be snatched by others more hard up than themselves.

But even those poor souls, one step from a jail cell or a nameless grave, found something here to nourish them. And, he thought, as he glanced down the tables of unbathed men and women with shabby dresser and holey socks, that for a moment at least they could escape into another world where all dreams were real and all hope had not been ground to naught.

Joseph walked into the reference room and over to the information desk.

A young woman seated behind the desk was trying to punch something up on the computer. The tip of her tongue was sticking impatiently out of the side of her mouth as she waited for whatever it was to appear on the screen.

"The perils of technology," she said, giving him a look of frustration. "When it works, the world is at your feet. When it doesn't, you're worse off than before."

"How come?" he asked.

"Because ever since last year we no longer put our new titles on index cards." She pointed to the computer with disdain. "They exist only inside its brain."

"Nothing is real unless it's on paper," he said.

"I keep telling them that," she replied and then she smiled. "What can I do for you?"

He took out his notebook and flipped through a few pages. "There's a word that needs looking up," he said.

"Our dictionaries are over there," she said, pointing to a nearby shelf.

"I tried," he said, jotting down the word on a blank page and then tearing it out. He showed it to her.

"'Polistes'," she said, glancing at it. "Sounds like a name— probably Latin."

"I suspect it is," he said. "But I tried a biographical dictionary, too, without any luck."

"Perhaps it's a technical term," she suggested. "Like a medical condition or a zoological genus. You can check those reference books over there." She pointed to a table.

He telephoned her hotel from the first pay phone on the street.

"Oh, Joseph! I'm so frightened!" Her voice was strained but it didn't seem terrified. From the sound of it, she could have seen anything from a mouse to the ghost of her dead father.

"What's wrong?"

"I drove back to my place to look for the photograph . . ." She stopped to catch her breath.

"And?"

"He was there!" A touch of panic came through.

"Take a deep breath Abby and relax. Now, take it slow. Who was there?"

"That man! The one who shot at us!"

"You saw him?"

"No! I saw his car! It was parked outside!"

"OK. Calmly," he cautioned. "Did he see you?"

"I don't think so. I didn't stop. As soon as I spotted him I got out of there as fast as I could!"

"You did the right thing," he said. "Wait in your room. I'll be over soon."

"Please hurry," she said. "I don't want to be left alone."

The Park Lane wasn't more than a ten-minute walk from where he called. He used the time to think.

Someone was after her, all right. And, by now, that someone had connected her to him. But what did they want? Were they trying to stop something from happening? Or were they trying to stop something from being found?

OK, he thought. Any of the above. But what was Abby's relationship to this? She was working for a public interest law firm. Fine. Noble. They had just negotiated a compromise with the timber interests. So who could object—besides the radical environmentalists? And, even so, what would they want with her? She was certainly a lesser enemy—if that.

He was mulling all this over in his mind as he entered the Park Lane.

And then we've got the boys on the third floor, he thought as he walked up to the elevator and punched number 5. They weren't here to sell scouting cookies. It wasn't like falling into a convention of Rotarians, either. No, it was more like the operations room at Cape Canaveral just before launching an intergalactic starship. Or, more to the point, the war room of a competing power that was planning to take over the controls.

But in Portland? Oregon?

He got off at the fifth floor and walked over to her room. He knocked at the door.

The door swung open. He saw her face streaked with thin, white stains. She threw herself into his arms.

"I don't know who to turn to!" she said.

He felt slightly embarrassed. A moment later, so did she. She backed away slightly and brushed away a tear. "I'm sorry," she said.

"Don't apologize," he replied. "I'm amazed you're holding up so well. You've been through a lot in the last few days."

"So have you," she said, walking over to a dresser and opening it up.

"For me it's just a story," he said. "I could walk away."

She turned and looked at him hard. "Could you really?"

"Well, maybe not," he admitted. "But my father's not involved."

"What if he was?" she asked.

132

"He couldn't. He's dead." And suddenly he thought of the young woman he followed to the art school yesterday.

Abigail pulled a bottle from the dresser drawer. "I picked this up downstairs. Get yourself a glass. There's one in the bath."

He went into the bathroom and found what he was looking for. He brought it out. She poured him a whisky and one for herself.

He watched as she tilted the glass and emptied half of the liquid into her mouth. "Be careful with that stuff," he said. "It's not milk."

"I don't want milk," she said. Her eyes had already started to turn red.

He took a small drink himself. "Yeah, well you also don't want a fuzzy head."

"Why not?" She looked at him defiantly and emptied the rest of the glass.

"Because we've got work to do!" he said, taking the bottle and rolling it under the bed. "And I don't want to do it all myself!"

She walked over to a chair by the window and let herself fall onto the seat. "I feel ill," she said.

"I don't wonder." He looked at her harshly. Perhaps too harshly, he thought. He tried to smile. It didn't go.

"Abby," he said, "I think I know where your father put what he was hiding."

She stared at him through her woozy red eyes. "Where?" she asked, softly.

"At his cottage."

"But . . ."

He held up his hand. "I know. It's wrecked. But they haven't touched the place I think it's hidden. Your father gave you the clue when he sent you that slip of paper."

"'Polistes'—but what does it mean?"

"I looked it up. In a scientific encyclopedia. It's a genus of insect. A most appropriate one for the Papyrus Club, I should add . . ."

"What is it?"

"A paper wasp. The article I read called them a miniature

133

organic paper factory. They chew up tiny bits of wood and use the pulp to build their nests." He gave her a significant look.

Her hand went to her mouth. "The wasp nest! Above his door!"

"That's right," he said.

Chapter 18

He went there alone, taking her car. He told her to go down to the hotel lobby, to have a coffee, relax but to keep her eyes and ears open. Something was being plotted from the third floor of the Park Lane and he wanted to know what.

As for himself, he made the drive to Meade with more than a little trepidation. It wasn't only the man in the tan Mercedes. Even worse for him were the wasps.

The first time it had happened to him was on a trip to Holland. He was camping in a park when he was stung. Within minutes his arm began to swell. In a half hour, the swelling had reached his shoulder and his heart was pounding so rapidly that he knew something had to be done. By the time he reached the hospital, he was in a state of shock. According to the doctor who treated him, the allergic reaction was so severe that ten minutes more and he might have been dead.

In the future, he was told, whenever he went camping, he was to take a dose of atropine along. So he never went camping. It was as simple as that.

Now he was going to meet some wasps without even the pleasure of nooning in the sun. In fact the sun was beginning to set. He wondered if wasps went to bed early in Portland or if they got particularly angry if someone stuck a hand into their house.

Polly had once pointed out a nest of wasps that had usurped a tiny portion of the overhanging roof. He who excused the life of flies and even of mosquitos, was bound to punish these intruders. He lay awake that night planning his attack. He made intricate sketches and copious notes. In the end he sprayed them with a high powered hose. It didn't seem to harm them at all. They just picked up their baggage and moved to the house on the other side of the fence. Which is why he rarely went into the yard—figuring they harbored a sense of revenge.

In short, unless he couldn't help it, he never went near a wasp and he hoped that vice was versa. But this was different. He was on a job.

Thus it was with a sense of trepidation that he drove into the confines of Meade campus and down the access road that led to the cottage by the brook. He half wished for the tan Mercedes to provide him with an excuse. But the parking lot here at Meade seemed to contain nothing even close—unless Mercedes had part ownership of Volkswagen.

He walked down the path to Bright's rustic cottage trying to make up his mind what to do.

Perhaps, he thought, paper wasps were different. Perhaps they only chewed wood. Maybe they had paper wings and paper jaws for paper bites. On the other hand, maybe they papered their house with death notices of people that they offed. He didn't put it past those evil little beasts. Not by a long shot.

The rushing brook that ran by the cottage provided a gentle counterpoint to his murderous thoughts. He walked to the door and glanced at the cornice above his head. He saw it. Or what looked like it, anyway. They were quiet. Too quiet. Something, he thought, was up.

He considered the idea that they might have had advance warning, that information had been passed to them by their scouts. They could have been waiting for him around the corner armed with their lethal missiles filled with toxin that would swell up his body like a overblown balloon until he exploded spewing mutant wasp virus that would eventually take over the world, even his wife and kids.

He peeked around the corner to see if anyone was there. No one was. There was only a rake. He grabbed it by the handle and decided that if he was going to do it, he might as well do it quickly and get it over with.

Walking back to the entryway, with the rake swung over his

shoulder, like a reluctant soldier, he stood there for a moment, took a deep breath, braced himself and then swung.

He missed, hitting the overhead porch light instead. The glass shattered around him. He looked down and saw all the tiny little bits.

He sighed, closed his eyes, took a breath and swung again. Bingo! It went flying. So did the wasps.

He ran. Down the side of the brook, up the path, over to the parking lot. He flew. The wasps in hot pursuit. Into the Volvo. And safe!

It wasn't until he heard the horrible buzzing that he realized the passenger window was gone. Blown out, he remembered, by a maniac's gun.

Out the other door. Down the path he ran. Along the brook back to the house.

He saw it glinting in the twilight. Next to the fallen nest. A few enemies buzzing around it. It had a shiny cover of bright red.

Swiftly flying past he got it on the run.

On up the path, along the brook again, back to the parking lot and into the car. He started it up and threw it in gear. He lurched forward, jamming his foot onto the gas, and then roared off. Leaving the little monsters behind. Except one.

It buzzed around the prize like the final guard of Porkchop Hill. He watched it, cautiously, out of the corner of his eye, as he drove. It hovered like a tiny warship above the little diary. Then, suddenly, quick as a flash, he took the diary and smashed it against the windscreen. He saw the remains ooze down the glass.

It was over. It was done. And he felt good.

He stopped at a little café on his way back—to celebrate, calm himself down and to see what it was exactly that he risked his life over.

Once inside the diner, he inspected it. He knew it was a diary from the bold black script over the red cover. He opened it up. It was written in the practiced hand of a school child. The first page contained a warning, written in firm caps:

He felt a tiny pang of intrusion as he paged through, reading
bits and pieces here and there. And then he came to a page
that was marked by the corner which had been folded down.
He began to read. It told about voices from the night. And it
told about smells. Horrible odors. It told of a girl sneaking
downstairs and seeing a man with half his clothes burned off, a
can seared to his blistered hand. It told of her father helping
the man. And it told of his face as he turned and saw the girl
staring, terrified at the sight of skin charred like a burnt roast
and the pain that oozed from the man's body like fiery plasma.
And it told of the man who grabbed her with a grip of steel
and looked at her like the devil himself who had come up from
the hell fires and said in a voice she would never forget that
she couldn't ever tell what she had just seen. No one. Not her
sister. Not her mother.

She saw his face glaring at her throughout the night—that
devil from the hell fire. And she was kept awake by the odor
of burnt skin and something else. Something that smelled like
gasoline.

He closed the book and then, rubbing the last trace of wasp
off the cover with his napkin, he put it in his pocket.

He sat there a while, in that small café, and thought. He
thought of Katherine/Tara and of sister Camilla. And he
wondered what seeds planted in a tender mind might grow
into.

Then he got up and drove back to the library.

When he got there he found the index to the local daily and,
using the date from the diary, made his search. He jotted down
the reference number and then sent for the microfilm.

After he received it, he seized an available machine and
wound the spool of celluloid through the weeks and months
until he found what he was after.

The article told about a fire and a delay in reimbursement
by an insurance firm. It quoted an investigator for the company
as saying, "Any fire of unknown origin is suspicious. Any
conflagration which totally destroys a business suffering severe

138

financial difficulties merits investigation." Joseph recognized the name of the insurance investigator who had been quoted.

Making a copy of the article, he went to a phone booth and placed a call. She wasn't in her room so he asked that she be paged in the lobby.

"Is that you?" she said, answering the phone.

"Yes. I found it. Right where I thought."

"What was it?"

"The diary of a child. If some of its contents were corroborated by an adult, it could blow McCullough's enterprise sky high.

"How soon will you be here?" she asked. "There's really something going on. I've been sitting in the lobby for the last hour watching them go in and out. It's like a beehive right before the birth of a new Queen."

He grimaced. "I wish you'd used another analogy."

"Where are you now?" she asked.

"I went to the library to look something up. I need to stop back at my hotel. There's some notes I want to collect."

"Well hurry up," she said.

He hung up. Then he stuck another quarter in the slot and dialled again.

He heard the voice of Hal when he was connected. "Tonight the moon will fill the sky. Mars will burn red. The winds will blow hot. The wolves will howl. The stars will bode great changes. Be aware. Many will run. But their feet will not touch the earth."

"I hope that's not meant for popular consumption," said Joseph.

"It's meant for those who are in touch."

"I have something for you," said Joseph. "Meet me at my hotel in half an hour."

"I have work myself tonight," said the electronic voice.

"It's now or never," Joseph warned. "It relates to Tara."

Chapter 19

He drove back to the Cambridge Arms, parking the Volvo on the street around the corner. The twilight had turned to darkness. He looked up. The moon was behind a cloud but the sky was light. For all he knew, the moon could have been full.

Walking inside, he went to the cubbyhole bar and had a quick scotch before going to reception.

"Any messages?" he asked.

The elderly woman looked in his box and pulled out a slip of paper. She handed it to him.

"Oh, Mr Radkin," she said. "By the way. You have a visitor . . ."

He was looking at the note. "I'm sorry," he said, glancing back up at her. "I didn't get that."

"Your father," she continued. "He looked quite ill, I'm sorry to say. So I gave him your key and told him to have a lie down in bed till you got back."

"My father?"

"Yes. I gathered you weren't expecting him. I hope it's not too much of a surprise."

"I can assure you, it is," he said, turning around and heading to the stairs.

The note he had put in his pocket read, "Mr Radkin, please call Camilla McCullough." At the bottom was a number.

He would have liked to have called when he got in, except for the fact that there was a visitor waiting for him. His father. At least that's what the woman at reception told him.

So he stood at the door, wondering what the proper decorum was on such occasions. How should he act? A smile and "Hi, dad. How's it feel to be back?" Or a serious facade. "Good to see you alive again, old man."

He gave a knock thinking that a warning was the least that he could do.

There was no response.

He put the key into the latch and turned the knob. The door opened. He walked in.

There was a man on the bed. It wasn't his dad. He felt only slightly disappointed.

He went over to the figure. He could hardly recognize him as the same grotesque man he had seen on the plane just days before. The man was breathing shallow breaths. He could hardly lift his hand. But it seemed he was trying to motion for Joseph to come closer.

Walking up to the bed, Joseph bent down on his knee and loosened Armstrong's tie and opened up his shirt. It was then he saw the blood oozing from his chest.

Armstrong wanted to say something. Joseph could tell. But all that came out of his mouth were bubbles.

"Don't try to talk," Joseph said. "I'll call for an ambulance."

Armstrong reached up, with what seemed to be his last ounce of strength and grabbed Joseph by his collar. He pulled him close. Close enough for him to smell his breath.

"The ship . . ." he began. He seemed to run out of air.

"You're the one who sent me that shipping schedule, weren't you? And you sent me the card for the Park Lane Hotel through that young art student. What's it about, Armstrong?"

"You're being used, son . . ." The words came out in a gravelly whisper.

"How come?"

But Armstrong didn't answer. That was all he said. That was all he ever said.

Joseph called reception.

"That man you let into my room is not my father. He's been shot in the chest. Call for an ambulance." But, in fact, Joseph knew it was too late for an ambulance. Armstrong was dead. Just like his father.

Then grabbing his notes and all his stuff, he threw them into his valise. He was about to leave the room when he noticed a camera case that Armstrong had left there. Quickly unzipping it, he saw that it contained some fancy, high tech stuff. Electronic gear, infra-red adaptor, telescopic lens. He checked the back. It was loaded with fresh film. There was also a roll at the bottom of the case that was used.

Pocketing the used roll of film, he zipped the case back up and slung it over his shoulder. Then he grabbed his valise and left.

He bumped into Wolenski in the lobby just as he was giving the bellboy an envelope and twenty bucks. "Bring this to a man named Nickels," he told the bellhop. "He works at the daily—city desk. It's just a few blocks."

The kid stared at the twenty and said, "I just hand him this? That's all?"

"Yeah."

"If it's drugs, it'll cost you fifty," the kid said.

Joseph took out another ten and gave it to him. "It's a roll of film. Just do it fast."

The kid saluted and went on the run.

Taking Wolenski by the arm, he rushed him out the door. "Come on!"

Wolenski offered no resistance till they were outside and then, glaring at Joseph with daggers, he reached into his pocket to get something to scream on.

Pointing a warning finger at him, Joseph said, "Look, there's a dead man in my room. The cops will be here any minute. So I don't have time for a yelling match. You can come with me to Willamette City or not. Maybe you can help. I doubt it. But it's your big chance for a story, hotshot . . ."

As Joseph was gathering steam for a second barrage, he suddenly saw something mouse-like stick its head out of Wolenski's pocket.

"Oh, no!" he said, "you didn't bring your dog!"

Wolenski shrugged.

Gritting his teeth and glaring at him for a second, he was about to say something else and then he decided that it wouldn't be worth it. "Just meet me in Willamette City by the lookout point going up to the bluffs—the one that overlooks the falls."

Then he ran off.

He jumped into the Volvo and started her up. What he didn't see was someone else who started up too. It wasn't Wolenski.

Chapter 20

The highway to Willamette City was well marked. You just
followed it along the river. From the far north of the city, you
drove past the grain elevators and warehouses full of wheat
and rice, past the freighters loading up with lumber for Japan
in trade for vast lots full of cars, past giant oil tankers and
barges filled with solid wastes searching for a dump.

And then, further on, the industrial landscape changed. Instead of rusty ships registered in Liberia, sleek yachts appeared
and boats for weekend sailors. Warehouses became offices. And
further still, the river became more wild.

He drove along the road that skirted the west side of the
river. When he reached the bridge that took him across to
Willamette City, he could see the *São Paulo* on the east bank,
some two hundred yards downstream to his left. Up above, on
the bluffs, the lights of the houses twinkled in the night. But
down below, besides the moon, there was only the occasional
street lamp sending a soft glow through the mist.

Crossing the bridge, he turned left along the shoreline and
drove up to the pier where the *São Paulo* was docked. Some
of the ship's lights were burning, enough to tell it wasn't
deserted. But there was no evidence of any work going on.

However, behind the cargo fence a long freight truck was
stationed with its loading door facing the ship's hold. The
diesel engine of the truck was idling, even though its lights
were off, so Joseph gathered that it was ready to move out.

Making a U-turn, Joseph headed south toward the falls. He
glanced at his watch. It was just a little after ten and the
business district was sound asleep. He noticed the municipal
elevator which he had taken last time to the top of the bluff

was closed for the evening. Even the café where he had met the old codger was shut. Everyone was tucked away nice and cosy upstairs, he guessed.

He drove down the road till he could see the falls. On the west side of the river he could see the mill, its smokestacks steaming into the night. Just below the falls, the loading pier for the blockhouse of McCullough Paper, Research Division, came into sight.

An old beat-up Toyota station wagon was parked outside the gate. Joseph pulled up next to it. Wolenski rolled his window down.

"Follow me," Joseph said, sticking his head through the passenger window of the Volvo which had been shot out.

He drove up to the top of the falls till he reached the lookout spot he and Abby had been to before. He parked the Volvo and got out, taking Armstrong's camera equipment with him.

The station wagon pulled up next to him.

"Nice view, huh?" asked Joseph, pointing down to the billows of white foam and spraying mists from the force of the rushing water as it plunged over the embankment, highlighted by the ivory glow of the moon.

From their vantage point they had a full look at the panorama. Far north, by the bend in the river, they could see the *São Paulo*. About a hundred yards downstream from the falls, on the west shore, was the mill. And fifty yards closer, on their side of the river was the blockhouse where the testing for the new pulp mill was going on.

They could see the blockhouse fine from where they were. The problem was, however, that the loading pier was obscured by the security fence and the surrounding brush.

"Unless I miss my guess," Joseph said, "the last load of whatever it is they're bringing should arrive in a few minutes." He took the camera out of the case and looked through the lens.

Then, handing it to Wolenski, he said, "Take a gander. Pretty professional equipment. With that lens you can snap a picture of anything, even in the dark."

Wolenski handed it back to Joseph and gave him a questioning look.

"I want to photograph the cargo that's coming in that truck."
Joseph pointed to the lorry he had seen before and which was
now making its way slowly toward the blockhouse loading pier.
"But in order to do it, I think I'm going to have to get right
down to the edge of the falls."

He looked to see whether Wolenski had understood him. "I
could use your help," he said. "I'll be in a precarious position.
I'll need you to steady me."

Wolenski nodded.

"There's a little path here that goes down through the
brush," said Joseph indicating the clearing that he meant.
"Stay about ten feet behind me. I don't want to go over the
edge if you trip. It's a long way over those falls."

As they disappeared into the brush, following the rough path
to the bottom, a car pulled up and parked between the Volvo
and the station wagon. A man got out. He stretched his thick
arms and reached into his jacket. In the pale moonlight there
was the glint of steel as he pulled out his gun.

The path which Joseph and Wolenski followed seemed to
disappear half-way down. From then on they had to make their
way through the brush which grew more dense the closer they
got to the bottom.

They knew which way they were going, even though they
couldn't see through the brush. As the sound of the falls got
louder, they could feel the spray penetrating through the thick
vines and wild hedges, until, finally, with Joseph leading the
way, they broke through to the barren cliff.

They ended up on a ledge just overlooking the falls. Right
under them the water had picked up the speed of a torrent as
it plunged over the side, dashing onto the jagged rocks and
sending out billows of spray which washed over them.

Joseph sat himself down on the edge and leaned slightly
forward to test his view. From his position, it was just possible
to see the loading bay for the blockhouse—if he leaned forward
far enough.

"Hold onto my belt," Joseph said.

Wolenski grabbed hold, but the rocks they were on, which
were constantly splashed by the water, were too slippery for
him.

"Try moving slightly higher," Joseph suggested. "Above the spray."

Wolenski made his way around Joseph and then above. Here he was able to grasp a rigid vine with one hand while holding on to Joseph's belt with the other.

Joseph tried to lean forward again with Wolenski holding onto him in that way. He could just see the truck's loading door opening up.

Turning back to tell Wolenski it would work that way, he noticed something poking out of Wolenski's pocket. It was a pair of ears.

"You idiot! I can't believe you brought your fucking dog!" he shouted, unable to control the rage he now felt.

Wolenski looked down at the head which now was completely exposed and then glanced back at Joseph as if to say that he, himself, hadn't known the dog was there.

"Forget it!" said Joseph. "We haven't time to get him back up now—unless you want to throw him in the river. But it's only a fucking suggestion." The way he felt, he would have thrown Wolenski in, too, if he didn't need someone to hold his belt.

A gang of men had come out onto the loading pier now. And through the telescopic lens, Joseph could bring them into close-up.

There was a barge which was hooked up to a cable which ran the short distance from the pier to the blockhouse. Attached to the barge was a crane. The crane was being lowered as several workers began undoing the containers.

Even with the top of the containers now opened up, Joseph still couldn't make out the cargo. It was only until the crane started lifting it out and moving it onto the barge that he could plainly see what had been sent here from Brazil.

"I'll be damned!" he said, as he clicked off a couple of shots. "I'll be damned!"

It was wood. Pile after pile of logs. Not the kind he had seen here in Oregon. These were thin ones, narrow and straight, with a different kind of bark. But he had seen them before. He didn't know trees. He didn't know flowers. He even had a hard time telling a turnip from a parsnip. But he knew the trees they were unloading. And his brain was just beginning to piece it all together when something suddenly made it stop.

"Very slowly," said the voice. "Nice and easy. Just hand me the camera and any film you got . . ."

Joseph eased himself back on to the rock. He turned and saw a husky man who was edging himself up next to him with one hand held out. His other hand held a gun. The gun was pointed right at Joseph's head.

"I figured it was you who killed Bright," said Joseph, looking at the man's ugly face, restructured, he knew now, after a horrible burn. "It was a pretty lame effort trying to put the blame on some crazy lumberjack. But the cops must be near to figuring it out, too. They're not that dumb. They were closing in, weren't they? So you had to kill Armstrong to cover your tracks. How about Katherine? Was she one of your victims too? Or did McCullough set you up for it?"

"McCullough?" Haveck let out a laugh. "He's too soft. Couldn't bring himself to do what needed to be done. She knew how to twist him round her finger. Twisted so hard, she damn near squeezed the life out of him . . ."

"What do you mean?" asked Joseph.

Haveck motioned toward Wolenski with his gun. "You should have asked your friend," he said, edging closer to Joseph till he could touch the camera strap. "Just be a good boy and hand it over."

His grandmother had once told him, "When you run out of cards, all you got left is gumption." And he had always listened to his grandma.

"What you really want is Katherine's diary, isn't it?" said Joseph, jerking the strap and suspending the camera over the water. "It's not in here. But I know where it is. I can get it for you."

Haveck's face got uglier. "As far as I'm concerned, it can go over the falls with you." He squeezed the trigger of the gun just as Wolenski let out a whistle.

The little mut leapt an instant before the gun went off. In that fraction of a moment, Haveck's hand had jerked at the sight of the flying canine, which landed on his shoulder, sinking it's rodent-like teeth into Haveck's meaty arm.

Joseph went down, not from the bullet but from the sharp retort, his feet slipping on the wet rock. The camera went flying from his hand, hitting Haveck in the chest and knocking him off-balance.

Wolenski still gripped Joseph's belt. But Haveck, without anything to prop him up, went over the side, with the little dog still chewing, tenaciously, on his shoulder.

It happened fast. First they were sucked down into the whirlpools of foam, and bobbing up once, then twice, they were swept by the torrent over the falls.

It was a primal scream. Like the last wild ape from the depth of the forest. Joseph didn't know where it came from. But its echo filled the night with pain and horror.

Joseph looked around at Wolenski whose hand still clutched him, knuckles white. His face was ghost-like. His eyes stared out at the torrential waters pounding over the falls onto the jagged rocks and into the sluice gates which led to the pulp vats of the paper mill.

They climbed back up through the brush to the top of the slope where their cars were parked.

"I'm sorry about your dog," said Joseph, looking into Wolenski's sorrowful eyes.

He put his arm on Wolenski's shoulder. "What Haveck said back there—about Katherine squeezing the life out of her father—what did he mean?"

A little tear rolled down Wolenski's cheek.

"You guys were involved in something, weren't you? And you blew it . . ."

Wolenski didn't wait to hear the rest. He turned around, got into his car and started it up. Joseph watched the bedraggled car as it began moving down the hill. Then he climbed into the Volvo and followed the slow-moving station wagon as it wound its weary way through the deserted mill town.

Just before they reached the bridge, however, Wolenski pulled over to the side of the road. Joseph drove up behind him and saw Wolenski get out of his car and stand by the river.

Joseph got out of the Volvo and went up to him. Wolenski

was staring at something—though, at first, it wasn't clear what. It took a moment before Joseph saw the two bodies, one big, the other small, floating silently down the stream.

And then, before Joseph could stop him, Wolenski jumped in. He swam out to where the bodies were floating and, taking the dog in one hand, by the nape of the neck, began swimming back.

When he reached the embankment, Joseph reached down and took the little body from him. Then, grabbing onto Joseph's outstretched hand, Wolenski climbed out of the drink, his clothes sopping wet.

He was cold and shivering, but it didn't seem to matter. He took the dog gently in his arms and lay it in the back of the station wagon. Closing it up, he got into the driver's seat and, making a U-turn, started back up to the top again.

Joseph met him at the lookout point. Wolenski had already taken a shovel from the back of his car and had started digging in the soft soil by the edge overlooking the falls.

When he had dug as deep as he felt was needed, he went back to the station wagon and got the dog. He brought it to the fresh-dug grave and knelt down before it. He held the tiny body for a moment by his cheek and then he placed it down and covered it with the loose soil. After covering it to the top, he firmed the earth gently with his foot. Then he drew the name "Ludwig" in the dirt with his toe.

Joseph watched him as he went back to the station wagon. He took something out of a box and put it on. When he turned around, Joseph saw he was wearing something on his face. It looked like a gorilla mask.

Then Wolenski got into his beat-up car and drove off.

Joseph was to see his image one more time. And when he did, he would remember that ridiculous mask.

Chapter 21

He stopped at the roadhouse he had been to before. He thought it was appropriate to call her from there.

She answered the phone right away. It was her own private number, he guessed.

"Haveck is dead," he told her.

There was a silence. Then she said, "I knew it would end like this."

"Did you know about your sister's diary?" he asked.

"I knew she kept one—ever since she was a child," she replied.

"She wrote about seeing Haveck half-burned and stinking of gasoline after he set your father's mill on fire. Quite a trauma for a young girl, wouldn't you say?"

"Yes." It seemed to him her voice was calm. Too calm.

"What happened to her, Camilla?"

She let out a tormented laugh. "Why don't you ask my father? He loved her, you know. He loved her far more than he ever loved me. But she betrayed him and, for my father, loyalty always came before love. So he went to Stavos and Stavos told him about Dr Phelps and his cure. It was very effective, he said, for bringing children who had run away back to their senses. If you needed it done quickly. And father needed it done quickly, didn't he? So he sent Haveck to take her—willing or unwilling, he didn't care."

"What kind of cure?" asked Joseph.

"What kind of treatment brings a child back to someplace she doesn't want to be? You treat her like you'd treat a stubborn mare. You break her will. Drugs. Electric shock. Any device will do . . ."

"Surely your father wouldn't stand for that!" said Joseph.

Her voice was bitter. "No? My father wanted results, Mr Radkin. And he wanted them fast! There was too much at stake for him to get soft—even for a daughter that he loved very much. My father is a man who wants to win at any price. And the price he paid this time was . . ." She stopped. It was as if she couldn't go on.

"Was what?" Joseph asked. "Did she kill herself, Camilla?"

"If she did, who could blame her?" she said.

"Did she? Do you know for certain?"

"All I know for certain is that a black cloud has fallen on this house, Mr Radkin. Things have been done which can never be forgiven."

Joseph took out his notebook and jotted something down in it. "You do realize you're talking to the press, don't you?" he said.

"Of course! I have your card. Why do you think I called you?"

"Why?"

"Because I want my father crucified!" she shouted.

He contacted Nickels at his home and arranged to meet him at the offices of the paper.

"You've been real decent," he said to Nickels when he got there. "Whatever I've got you can have. Use it any way you want. I just need to write up my story and fax it off to Saunders before midnight."

Nickels gave him his desk and access to his VDU. "The fax room is around the corner," he said. "By the way, I had that film developed. Whose was it?"

"A guy named Armstrong. An insurance investigator. He was the one who originally had the case of the McCullough mill fire."

"Some bulldog!" said Nickels. "Never gave up, huh?"

"He was working for someone else now. The two cases linked up. So what was on the film?"

"That freighter from Brazil. It was unloading logs here in Oregon! Can you beat that?"

"I can't beat it, but I think I can explain it," Joseph said. "I

152

don't know trees. But I know that one. It grows all over where I live. Eucalyptus. You don't see it up here because it needs a temperate climate—something you ain't got. Anyway, they're growing it in Brazil. Got big plantations of 'em, I understand. They grow real fast. You can harvest every four years."

"What do they use it for?" asked Nickels.

"To make paper. The pulp is naturally white. So you don't need to bleach it." Joseph gave him a significant look.

"So that was why the dioxin report came out nil?"

"On the button! They're not using a new bleaching agent. They're switching over to a new kind of wood!"

Nickels raised his eyebrows. "But one that isn't grown in Oregon."

"Which means you don't need to cut down any forests. That ought to make the environmentalists sing a little victory tune."

"The environmentalists don't run this state, Radkin," said Nickels shaking his head. "The lumber industry does."

Joseph glanced at his watch. "I've got an hour to finish my story and fax it off," he said.

"I'll catch you later," said Nickels. "I'm going to bed."

He finished with thirty seconds to spare. He fed it through the fax machine and that was that.

But something didn't feel right. There were pieces that didn't match. And there were a few things left undone.

He took a card out of his wallet and studied it. Putting it down on the desk, he thought a moment as he drummed his fingers.

There was only the office number on the card, but he figured calls would be forwarded at night. A man like that was bound to have emergencies. Anyway, he hoped he was right.

Picking up the phone, he dialled for an outside line. He waited as it rang. There was a clicking sound and then the ringing suddenly had a change in pitch. Someone connected on the other end.

"Yeah?" It was a male voice. Joseph pictured the man in the cowboy boots he had seen at Stavos' house the other day.

"This is Mr McCullough," said Joseph, dropping his voice

153

an octave. "I know it's late, but it's very important that I speak with Mr Stavos. Tell him it's of the utmost urgency."

· "Wait a second," said the voice. He heard the sound of the receiver being dropped on something hard.

A few minutes later another voice came on the line. It was more modulated than the one before. "This is Stavos. What's the problem, Mr McCullough?"

"Don't hang up, Mr Stavos," said Joseph, "it's important that you hear me out. It's very likely that McCullough will soon be brought up on charges of fraud and arson—if not murder. It's also possible that your name will come up in the investigation. On the other hand, it might not. It all depends on what you have to say."

"Who is this?" The voice was brusque.

"Someone who believes you're being framed."

"I don't know what this is all about," said the voice on the other end of the line, "My dealings with McCullough were only advisory."

"How so?"

"He needed a safe place for someone to stay—somewhere close but unobtrusive. I suggested he contact a colleague who had some cottages outside of town that were available."

"How was McCullough referred to you in the first place?"

"Through his daughter."

"You mean Katherine?"

"No. I think her name's Camilla . . ." There was a brief silence. Then Stavos said, "Listen, I'm not responsible for how people treat their children."

"I guess not," Joseph replied. "But you're always there with your scrub brush when they need you to clean up the mess, am I right?"

"I suppose you could say that . . ."

"Except I didn't mean it as a compliment. Frankly, Stavos, I don't much care for exorcists," said Joseph. "Shepherds who bring lambs back to the fold usually end up delivering them for slaughter."

"Then perhaps you'd care to spend a weekend with Reverend Moon," said Stavos, acidly.

"No thanks," said Joseph. "But if he were still alive, maybe you'd like to spend a month with Senator McCarthy."

He hung up the phone. Then he picked it up again and placed a call to Abby.

"You still awake?" he asked.

"Are you joking?" she said.

He told her what had happened.

"So Katherine gave her journal to my father. And he used it to blackmail McCullough?"

"It sure seems that way. But there's something that doesn't make sense . . ."

"What's that?"

"The new pulp mill. If I've got my information straight it would have been as ecologically sound as they get. And the trees they'd use wouldn't come from Oregon's forests."

"My father probably didn't know . . ."

"Yes. I realize that. But it still doesn't feel right to me."

"It doesn't have to feel right to be right, does it?"

"To me it does." He thought a moment. "I'd still like to see that photo, if you can find it. The one of the Papyrus Club."

"Now?"

"You have plans tonight?"

"You've got the car," she said. "Come over to the hotel and pick me up."

He drove the Volvo with the shattered window, compliments of Haveck he knew now, to the Park Lane Hotel.

It was quiet on the streets. Just a few lacy clouds stood between him and the full moon. He looked up and saw a shooting star. And in his mind he heard the words: "Tonight the moon will fill the sky. Mars will burn red. The winds will blow hot. The wolves will howl. The stars will bode great changes . . ."

He didn't believe in all that crap. But it did make him wonder.

There wasn't much happening in the lobby as he pushed his way through the glass door of the hotel. The bar had shut down for the night. Only a sleepy bellhop was stationed by the registration desk. He nodded. The bellhop frowned.

It was more from curiosity than anything else that made him do it when he got inside the elevator. He pushed the button marked 3 instead of 5. He felt himself being lifted upward. And then the elevator stopped.

The door opened and he looked outside. It was a different world here. It could have been running on Tokyo time or London or New York. Silk-suited men were walking through the halls, drinks in hand, ties loosened, having loud discussions. Electronic noises in the background. And then:

"You got the wrong floor again, bud!"

It was the same bozo as before. The tough hall guard.

"My mistake," Joseph smiled.

"Don't keep making it too often," growled the guard.

"Guess I'm just automatically attracted to the loudest parties, that's all," said Joseph, giving him a shrug.

"This one's private!"

"And long," said Joseph. "You get any sleep around here?"

The guard seemed to loosen up a bit. "Not much, buddy, I'll tell you that. But if things go right, we'll clear out tomorrow and you can come down here as much as you want."

Saying that, the guy walked over to the elevator and stuck in his hand. "Five, wasn't it?"

Joseph nodded.

The guard pushed the button, the door closed and Joseph went up again.

Abby was dressed in casual slacks and a blouse that matched her hair. She looked wide awake when he came in.

"I was able to get the names of some of the people on the third floor," she said.

"How's that?" he asked.

She winked, slyly. "Amazing what you can find out hanging around bars."

"Yeah," he agreed. "You can get a real education."

"For example, Portland this week seems to be an international meeting ground for some very important persons."

"For instance?"

"Not ones you'd recognize, I'd dare say."

"Try me," he said.

"Well, there's Jeffrey Conrad Martin, for starters."

He shook his head. "I guess you got me. Nice name though."

She gave him a satisfied smile. "So you don't know everything."

"Did I ever say that?"

"Not in so many words. Anyway, Mr Martin is chairman of Martin, Dean and Marriott, a leading investment group. Would you like to guess what they specialize in?"

"Buyouts?"

She looked a little crestfallen. "How did you know that?"

"I thought it was obvious. Wasn't it?"

"I suppose it was."

"Who else?"

"Christopher Hartman."

"Another name from the corporate hall of fame?" Joseph asked.

"You clearly don't hang out in the right circles. Otherwise you'd know that he vies with Michael Milken for Prince of the Junk Bonds."

He sat down in a chair. "I guess the list goes on and on."

"It's a vultures' banquet," she said. "Organized by Felix Tobias, the King of Arbitrage. Millennium Industries is nothing more than a front group for an investment cartel, by the way. And all the talk is just about one thing . . ."

"Shoot it to me softly," he said, feeling more tired than he thought.

"Paper."

"I bet."

"So it's all pretty simple," she continued. "There's a take-over planned for McCullough Paper. All the electronic gadgetry is hookups to brokerages and other houses of finance. They're buying up the stock."

"Nothing is simple," he said. "Sure they're planning a takeover. But why now? And why McCullough?"

"They must be vulnerable," she said.

"That's not the half of it." He ran his fingers through his hair. "I don't feel good," he said. He didn't look good either.

"I don't wonder," she replied. "How many dead bodies have you seen in the last few hours?"

"It depends on whether you count dogs and wasps." He got up. "Let's go," he said.

"You certainly must want that photo awfully bad. What do you expect to find out?"

He looked at her strangely. "Frankly, I'm afraid to think about it."

He gave back her keys. She drove. The breeze was stiff.

"I'll have to get that window fixed," she said.

He felt the bandage on his face. "Why don't you keep it that way. As a memento."

It wasn't far to her place. No more than ten minutes. In fact, they could have walked.

She parked the car across the street and looked over at her house. "It will never be the same again," she sighed.

"Nothing ever is," he said.

"I was brought up in Europe," she said. "Did I tell you that? I found a sense of history there. I gained a preference for the old over the new . . ."

"The world is going backwards," he said. "America is old now. Europe is new."

"But Europe doesn't have the forests," she said.

"That's true. It doesn't have the forests."

They got out of the car and walked up to her front door.

She looked at him with sadness. "I loved this house once. Now I'm almost afraid to go inside."

"You'll love it again. After you clean it up."

She opened the door and it all came rushing back to her.

"Would you like me to go? Just tell me where it is."

"I'll go," she said. She took a deep breath and walked in.

Nothing had changed. It wasn't a bad dream. The place was still trashed.

She walked through the broken memories lying shattered on her floor till she came to an oaken cabinet. The drawers were pulled out and had been thrown upside down onto the floor. Lifting them one by one, gently, she stacked them against the wall and then went back and sifted through the scattered contents.

She found a large manila envelope at the bottom of the pile.

It had been torn in half. She emptied both parts and sorted through the pictures. Finding the pieces of the one she wanted, she made a space on the floor and set them down so they fit back together. "The Papyrus Club," she said.

He got down on his hands and knees and inspected it.

"The man in the middle is my father," she said quietly. "The fellow to his left looks very much like a younger Felix Tobias. He's got the same butterfly mark."

"That mark on his forehead," said Joseph, "it's not a butterfly. It's a wasp. That's why they called him 'Polistes'."

She looked down at the photo of the man on the right. "I don't know who the other one is, though." She glanced at Joseph. "Do you?"

He was staring at the photo. He was deep in thought. "I'm sorry to say I do," he replied.

Chapter 22

He felt very fatigued. Something in the corner of his mind kept asking him to listen, but it was as if his ears were filled with bits of paper.

"Is there something wrong?" she asked.

"There is something wrong. There's a lot wrong. But I'm tired and it's hard for me to think."

"Should I take you back to your hotel?"

"I've checked out," he said.

"Then come to mine."

Perhaps the world's axis had shifted a little, he thought. Everything seemed to be off balance to him. Not strictly perpendicular.

There was an echo in the air from the wind whipping through an empty garbage can. There was the sound of footsteps in the night. The footsteps were theirs, but in his mind they were magnified and out of sync. He heard strange noises coming from his head. Electrical hums and buzzings. Computers and wasps. Maybe Mars was red tonight, he thought.

There was an eerie feeling in the hotel when they got back. It was like the first scene of a monster film when all you have is mood but you knew damn well that something awful was going to happen next.

They went to the elevator and waited for it to open up. He watched the semicircular dial on top move down from four to three to two. It opened up. They got in. He pushed three. She looked at him.

The lift went up and then it stopped. The door opened. The

guard was there. But it was quiet. Very quiet. You could have heard a martini glass drop.

"Hi," said Joseph, giving a little wave. "Just thought I'd say goodnight before I turned in."

It was clear the guard had been nodding off. His eyes were swollen.

"Everyone asleep?" Joseph asked, sticking his head out and glancing down the hall.

"Not likely," said the guard. "If anyone sleeps, it's just with one eye shut."

Joseph glanced at his watch. It was two o'clock. "Just three more hours," he said.

"Till what?" The guard opened his sleepy eyes wider and stared at him.

"Till the east coast wakes up."

There were two single beds, which was all right by him. But he was so tired he would have slept on the floor. After all, the rug was soft.

He slipped off his trousers and his shirt and his shoes, leaving on his underwear and socks. He got into bed and crawled underneath the covers.

"Goodnight," he said.

"Goodnight."

Very early in the morning he heard the roar. It sounded like the final cheer at the superbowl game. He glanced at his watch. It was 5.30 a.m. Then he went back to sleep.

He dreamed that the winds were hot and flames leapt from the forest.

He heard a voice. He thought it was a scream.

"It's ten o'clock. There's a lot happening in the world today. You ought to get up."

He opened his eyes. Abigail was standing before him dressed in a frock. She was holding a tray.

"I had this sent up," she said, putting the tray down on a three-legged table.

On the tray was orange juice, toast, two eggs, ham, marmalade and coffee. There was also the morning paper. Joseph took the morning paper and sat up. He unfolded it and scanned the front page. His stomach sank.

The lead story was the scandal at McCullough Paper, how they had claimed to have removed dioxin from the bleaching process when, in fact, they were secretly bringing logs up from Brazil which made pulp that didn't need to be bleached. The adjoining article was about the reopening of the investigation concerning the McCullough lumber mill fire.

Joseph put the paper down and gave her a look as if he had been handed prunes on the tray instead of ham and eggs.

"I thought you'd be pleased," she said. "Isn't that your story?"

He showed her the paper. "Yeah, it's my story," he said. "But it came through the wire service. It probably hit New York in time for the morning edition. But even if it didn't, every brokerage firm in the country has a direct line to the news agencies. They all had access to it."

"That means you got national coverage. Isn't that what you wanted?" She looked at him curiously.

He pulled the covers off and threw on his shirt and slacks. Then he grabbed the phone and made a call.

"Correct me if I'm wrong," he said to Nickels when he came on the phone. "The stock of McCullough Paper fell dramatically this morning. A bunch of money flooded in and bought them up."

"Be at the Park Lane at noon," said Nickels. "There's a press conference scheduled by the new owners."

"Millennium Industries?"

"The very one."

He hung up the phone and looked at her. "I'm going downstairs," he said.

"What about your breakfast?" she asked.

"I don't think my stomach could take it. I need to find out what's going on."

She located him at the bar. He was already on his third drink.

"Did you find out what you wanted?" she asked.

"I'm afraid I already know," he said. He motioned to the bartender and held up his glass.

She looked at him askance. "What are you drinking?"

"Double scotch."

"In the morning? On an empty stomach?"

He looked at his watch. "It's almost noon."

"Won't you tell me what's going on?" she asked.

"You'll find out soon enough," he said.

The press conference was held in the Cornelius Suite of the hotel. It was a fancy meeting room with a lush carpet, velvet drapes and crystal chandeliers—though they were probably fake, he thought.

There was a small stage in front with a long table. Sitting at the table were some of the men Joseph had seen on the third floor. Standing by the dais was Polistes—otherwise known as Felix Tobias.

The place sat about fifty. Maybe seventy had crammed in.

It had already started when they arrived. They stood at the back, next to a man whom Abigail knew well.

"Hello, Henry," she said.

He nodded. "Hello, Abigail."

Tobias was just concluding his statement.

". . . so, allow me to sum up. Millennium Industries has faith in Oregon. We want what you want—a thriving economy. And we know the future holds good things in store for the people here. Remember, what we see as our western frontier, Asia sees as its eastern rim. The next decade will belong to the Pacific. And Oregon, with its magnificent harbors, its natural resources and its enterprising spirit will lead the way. The great Northwest is no longer America's hinterland. It is the new Gold Coast—or soon will be."

There was a scattering of applause and then Tobias said, "OK. Let's open it up to questions."

"What about this idea of bringing coals to Newcastle," someone shouted out. "Or in this case, trees from Brazil . . ."

There were some titters.

"Pretty lousy notion, wasn't it?" said Tobias. "Makes no economic sense."

"But it did make environmental sense," someone else shouted.

"We respect the environment—but we respect your economy too."

Another shout. "What plans do you have for the new pulp mill?"

"It's been temporarily scrapped," said Tobias.

There were some murmurs.

"We need time to reorganize," Tobias added. "We'll keep you well informed of our plans, however."

"Will you guarantee continued employment?" someone asked.

"In the long run there will be more jobs," Tobias answered. "There will be some short-term rationalization, however. We need to rebuild this operation from the ground up so it will be fit and trim and competitive in the world market . . ."

"Bullshit!" someone shouted out. It was Joseph.

Everyone turned around and looked at him.

"Isn't it true, Mr Tobias, that you don't give a fuck about Oregon or jobs or the environment? Isn't it true that what you're really interested in is a quick buck?"

Tobias turned to someone at his left and said, "Who is that man?"

Joseph continued shouting. "How much did you pay for McCullough Paper, Mr Tobias? A hundred million? Two hundred? Four? A billion dollars? And how did you finance it?"

"Can we go on?" asked Tobias pounding on the table. "Will someone get this man out?"

"Wasn't it a leveraged buyout, Tobias?"

Someone grabbed him by the shoulder. It was the elevator guard. "I thought there was somethin' funny about you," he said.

But Joseph didn't hear him. He kept shouting. His face was bright red. "Why doesn't someone ask how he's going to pay back the debt?"

The guard pulled at his arm. Joseph broke loose. "I'll tell you how!" he yelled. "He's going to sell every goddamn tree he can get his hands on to Japan! At two thousand bucks a shot! It's called asset stripping, folks! And these guys are masters at it!"

Grabbing Joseph around the neck in a stranglehold, the guard said, "That's all, buddy."

Abigail looked at him horrified. She seemed to have no idea what was going on.

"Ask him about your fucking agreement!" Joseph shouted at Henry Mellon, as the guard dragged him out. "Ask him!"

Abigail turned to Mellon and glared. "Are you going to ask him or not?"

Up on stage, Tobias seemed just slightly shaken, but not much. He straightened his tie. "I'm sorry for the interruption," he said.

"There was an agreement reached with McCullough Lumber regarding Bear Creek," Mellon called out. "I trust the new owners will abide by its terms . . ."

"We're eager and willing to talk with anyone about any of our new properties or leases," said Tobias. "We'll take all views into consideration."

"Mr Tobias, are you saying the agreement is off?" Abigail shouted.

"No. I'm saying that we must reconsider all decisions made by the former management in the light of new economic realities."

"Are you going to cut Bear Creek?" she shouted. "Tell us!"

"There are over a hundred thousand acres of land that Millennium Industries now controls. I can't account for every parcel, here and now. But I will promise that all decisions regarding use will be fully discussed with the appropriate parties legitimately interested in these matters . . ."

"That sounds fair," said Mellon.

Abigail turned to him with fire in her brilliant eyes. "Henry," she said, "you're a fool! You always were and you always will be!"

And with that she stomped out.

Chapter 23

They packed up their stuff and Abigail checked out of the hotel and drove home. He went along with her.

"Is there any hope of getting a new injunction?" he asked.

"Possibly," she replied. "It would take a few weeks, at the very least. The Oregon court would turn it down. We'd have to appeal to the 5th circuit in San Francisco."

He rubbed the side of his head where he felt a little pain was starting to grow. "Someone told me that in two weeks they could have the entire forest cut down."

"It's true," she said.

She parked across the street and looked out. The fine old house cast a thick shadow in the afternoon sun. On both sides the empty lots, now cleared of all debris, seemed to accentuate its loneliness.

"In ten years this entire street will be filled with cracker boxes—town houses, they call them. They make them out of press board and glue. They prefabricate all the parts and they throw them together in a month—sometimes less.

"This house," she continued, pointing to her own, "probably took a year to build. It was constructed with pride and care." She turned to Joseph and gave him a sad, little smile. "Eventually it will be torn down, just like the ones on either side. Not because it was poorly built or designed. But simply because it's uneconomical. Or at least that's how they justify it."

"I'll tell you something about economics," he said. "It's just a clever rationale for why some people have things and why others don't and why some things are built and why others are torn down. It has nothing to do with the preservation of forests or fine old houses."

"You think so?" she asked. She looked a little worn down, he thought.

"Come on," he said, "I'll help you clean up."

They went inside and started clearing things away, putting as much as they could into a shed in the back garden. They swept up the bits and pieces of plastic and wood and smithereens of glass, filling a dozen plastic sacks. The rest of the things that were salvageable, they stacked in neat piles on the floor.

It was when they were fitting a tarpaulin on the remnants of the greenhouse dormer to keep out the rain that they first heard them.

The sound filled the air like a thousand sheets flapping on a giant clothes line. They looked up into the sky and saw a darkening cloud.

"Why are there so many helicopters up there?" she asked.

"Steel locusts," he said. "They're heading south."

She looked at him curiously. "What do you mean?"

"Does your television still work?" he asked.

"I don't know," she replied. "Let's bring it in and see."

They brought her portable Sony into the kitchen and hooked it up. She went to hustle something for them to eat while he fiddled with the dials.

The picture which he brought into view was an overhead shot of the forest.

". . . the setting for this confrontation between nature and machine couldn't be more spectacular. That bit of crystal blue to the southeast is Bear Creek Lake. Just north of it is the old logging road. I take it, that's where you are, Jim . . .?"

The screen showed a close-up of a man in a red hunting jacket holding a microphone.

"That's right, Hank. And behind me the great goliaths of the forest are rolling into position. If you've never seen a John Deere Tree-Harvester in action before, you're in for a real treat. That sweetheart can run up to four trees through its delimber—and that's per minute! We've also got some mighty big cats down here fitted with feller bunchers. I understand each one of them can mow down several hundred trees an hour."

Flash to the whirly in the air.

"How about those other machines? From up here, it looks like an army!"

Back on ground again.

"You've got everything from whole-tree chippers that grind up smaller trees and blow the chips directly into forty-foot vans, to grapple skidders—them babies haul the bigger logs to the tractor trailers. And let me tell you something, Hank. I wouldn't want to be in front of one when it does!"

Cut to the whirly suspended in the air, looking down. The lush trees sparkling in the afternoon sun.

"Jane, you're by the Bear Creek Lodge with the pro-testers . . ."

A woman, blonde, dressed in a chic ski jacket. Her bright red fingernails glistening as her hand clutched the microphone. In the background were the lake, the lodge and knots of people holding picket signs reading "Save Our Forest".

"Right you are, Hank. Some of these people are pretty upset. They thought they had an agreement that Bear Creek wouldn't be cut for at least one year—a moratorium, they say, that would have given them time to lobby congressional support. Now, with the sale of McCullough Industries, that agreement seems to be null and void. And these people are hopping mad. Some of them, in fact, are prepared to put their bodies on the line . . ."

Back to the whirly.

"What does that mean, exactly, Jane?"

The ground.

"It means chaining themselves to trees and maybe even worse . . ."

The whirly.

"Worse?"

The ground.

"Yes, Hank. Worse. They call it monkey-wrenching. Others call it terrorist sabotage . . ."

The whirly.

"That's heavy stuff, Jane. We'll come back to you soon. But we have to stop here for a commercial break. We'll return to The Great Forest War in just a moment . . ."

Joseph turned off the sound as the sight of a dancing toilet roll came on screen.

She brought over a plate of crudités and cheeses and sat down with him. They watched, together, mesmerized by what they saw.

He was about to get up to turn on the volume when she held his arm. She shook her head. "Please, not the sound . . ."

It was a panorama of the wooded foothills from above. They saw the sky, the lakes, flocks of birds. A world at peace, or so it seemed.

Then, down below, the terrible machines, moving forward, inch by inch, yard by yard.

By the lodge, the protesters, dispersing now. Defying, it seemed, the police lines and barriers that had been set up.

Back above, a sudden flurry of black birds in the sky, like a swooping cloud or an uneasy omen of discontent.

Below the machines had left the logging road. Launching into the forest now, giant trees falling before them, silently thundering down. And, in its wake, tiny forest animals on the run. A squirrel, a fox, a covey of quail, a family of hare.

The harvesters moved forward, relentlessly. In their wake, the bodies of fallen trees lay, ready for the next machine, their branches to be severed, delimbed, shaved of bark, lifted up, harnessed, attached to sky hooks of the hovering helicopters, the metal locusts Joseph had first seen, and flown off. To where? he wondered. A waiting ship?

In the tracks of the goliaths, dug deep into the ground, the camera focused on the crushed body of a hedgehog. Perhaps it was Pogo, Joseph mused. Or a tiny dog.

And then the screen filled with images of protesters who had surrounded an ancient cove. Some had shackled themselves to trees, forcing the lumbering machines to temporarily halt while some husky policemen armed with metal hacksaws cut through the chains and dragged them off.

The camera chose a couple of young women to observe. They had locked themselves together to an elderly tree covered thickly with green moss. One, whose eyes were filled with tears, was a girl Joseph had seen his first day in Portland when he had visited Meade. Her name was Ginger. The other woman

169

was as tiny and as frail. But something about her seemed different as the camera focused in for a close-up and a microphone was thrust up to her mouth.

Joseph took out the photo he had carried in his pocket. The one Wolenski had given him of Tara. He showed it to Abigail. They weren't certain, but they thought it could be her.

The young woman had eyes of piercing blue that looked forceful and determined. Joseph turned the volume up as she spoke:

". . . there is nothing for us but to put our bodies on the line," she was saying. "You have left us no alternative. Today we are just hundreds and you will have our forest. But the earth is angry and the skies are growing dark. Tomorrow thousands will replace us, for they see where you have led. And the next day will come millions . . ."

Again the picture was of the machines, moving on, grinding through the underbrush, severing their giant prey like slender reeds or stalks of corn, as if they were not mighty trees at all which had survived five hundred years of fires and plagues, of lightning and storm. Surviving tall and strong anything that nature could throw at it. Except the steel arm of man.

They watched. The picket signs were crushed under heavy metal webs. Other chains were cut. The locusts swept up the trees in their mighty jaws. And flew them off.

They watched. The shadows grew long. The sky grew dark, and still the iron machines marched.

The floodlights were turned on. From below. From above. The forest was lit in a harsh and eerie artificial glow.

And the ferocious cutting continued.

A floodlight from above had focused on something. A single tree. The camera focused in.

Again he turned up the sound.

". . . it looks like—I really can't believe it! But, Hank, it looks like a gorilla!"

The camera focused closer now. High up in a magnificent Hemlock he sat. Two hundred feet up. Perhaps even three. He could almost touch the clouds.

More floodlights were turned on him. The beams were intense. The gorilla stood up and beat on his chest.

"Hank, it's a man. He's wearing a gorilla mask. We've got him covered in the spotlights, but I don't think the harvesters see him!"

The machines were only fifty feet away. On either side the trees were crashing down.

"He's just sitting on that limb, thumping his chest! The cutters are getting pretty near. We'll see if we can drop a rope ladder down to him."

Joseph had gotten out of his chair and had come up close.

"Is that Wolenski?" she asked him.

He nodded.

On the television, voices were shouting.

"We can't get to him! They're too close! It's crashing down! Oh, my God! It's crashing down! That guy is nuts!"

And then he heard it again. As the camera focused in on Wolenski one more time before he fell to earth. That terrible scream. It seemed to echo through the forest. As Mars turned red. And the winds blew hot. And somewhere something precious had come to an end.

Chapter 24

He telephoned Polly and told her he'd be home very soon. There were just a few things he had to finish up. Then he called Alaska Airlines and found out that the next plane left in a little over an hour. He also called Jane at *Investigations Magazine* and asked her to do a little research for him.

Abigail offered to take him to the airport.

"What are you going to do with yourself?" he asked her as they drove down the highway that ran ribbon straight across town.

"I'm not sure yet," she said. "But I want to go away for a while."

"Back to Europe?"

She shook her head. "I want to spend some time in the wilderness—while we still have some wilderness left."

"I knew a woman—Gerry's her name—who used to go up to the redwoods to commune with nature whenever things in her life shut down. She had a special tree that she'd camp under. Sometimes I think I'd like to do that. But I don't know how. I'm a city boy. I need lots of people around."

"Everyone knows how," she replied. "It's inside all of us, locked up in a secret recess in our head. My father said it's a kind of molecular imaging passed down through the generations."

"We all crave to go back to our ancestral home, is that it? Even if it's a tree."

"Something like that," she said. "It's a world of enormous beauty." She glanced at him. "Perhaps I could show it to you some day."

"Maybe," he said.

Neither of them spoke for a while. Then Abigail said, "I wonder about her sometime . . ."

"Who?"

"That young woman, McCullough's daughter, who gave my father her diary. I looked through it. Her images of the fire were terrifying. But there was also an undercurrent in the pages after the fire that were almost as frightening . . ."

"What do you mean?" asked Joseph.

"About father and daughter. Nothing explicit. Just the mood she established in her writing."

"There's another story, you know. About a man who met a young woman from a different class and became her teacher and influenced her to do something terrible and in so doing, lost the very thing he had come to love. I pieced it together, without really wanting to believe it," said Joseph. "But Tara helped spike the tree that killed the logger."

"How do you know?" asked Abigail.

"Haveck told me as much. But it all fits. It's a tactic that Wolenski approved of. And the land where it happened was leased to McCullough Lumber. McCullough was doing selective cutting then—lumberjacks with chain saws, not mechanical tree harvesters. The tree spikers probably sent a warning that was ignored. And when the lumberjack was killed—something they never expected would happen—Tara dropped out of sight. She must have been furious with her father—furious enough to give the diary to your dad."

"But how do you know it was her?" Abigail said.

"It's the only thing that makes sense. McCullough loved her too much to put her in the hands of a butcher like Stavos. But Camilla, her sister, was jealous enough to suggest it. McCullough, however, used Stavos to find a safe house for Katherine to hide—some cottages where Stavos' colleague, Dr Phelps, once had his clinic."

"Was it a safe house or a prison?"

"There's a thin line between protection and restraint, isn't there? Anyway, her father didn't want her found. But neither did Haveck. McCullough probably told Haveck to help her hide out. But Haveck became her jailer and would have killed her if she hadn't made her escape. Haveck thought

McCullough was weak—he knew the empire was crumbling and he was willing to murder in order to save it. But McCullough wasn't. In the end, blood truly is thicker than water."

"I still don't know how you're sure that McCullough's daughter was involved in spiking the tree," Abigail said.

"You mean short of a confession? There was one more bit of evidence that clinched it for me. The logger's widow. She said a woman appeared out of nowhere to pay off an insurance policy—one she never knew existed. Katherine had easy access to cash. And she used it as a form of restitution."

"Maybe," said Abigail. "Surely tactics like that weren't beyond them."

"They were foolish," Joseph replied, as they reached the terminal. "But they weren't villains."

"Frankly, I still don't understand what it was all about," she said as he got out. "Why my father was killed. I mean I understand some, but not everything."

"He was being used, Abigail. Just as I was used."

"For what?"

"Ultimately, to make some people rich. But there's something else. Something I don't know yet. I still haven't put it all together."

"Maybe you don't have all the pieces yet."

He nodded in agreement. "Maybe not."

The flight back to San Francisco wasn't as bad as the one he had taken coming there. It was smoother weather. But it was also because he was deep in thought.

When he had first started training as a journalist, a seasoned veteran who later became a friend had told him to watch out for people with hidden agendas. Like the CIA. They liked to plant stories, he said, with creditable reporters who then would write them up. The next day, like a boomerang, they would find their articles coming back to them through the wire service. Overnight, hearsay had become established fact. It was blind journalism, he said. Inexcusable. And it usually came from laziness—from not wanting to follow things up.

Joseph had always been very sensitive about that. He had

always been careful about his sources, trusting only his own eyes and ears.

This time it had been different. Though he hadn't really been doing a story. Just collecting information—most of which was handed out to him.

But what had been handed out to him? And who had done the handing?

And what was the result?

He called Jane from the airport when he arrived.

"I have that information you wanted," she said. "That piece of land is owned by the Federal Government. It's controlled by the Forest Service. But very recently an Oregon lumber company put in a bid to cut it."

"If anyone ever calls me a fool again, agree with them," he told her.

"I always do," she said.

He placed another call when she hung up.

"Welcome back," said the voice after he was connected. "You did a great job!"

"I want to see you," said Joseph.

"It's late," said the voice.

"I don't care if it's late," Joseph replied. "I want to see you now!"

The house still appeared to be smiling when the taxi left him off and he walked up the path. Only this time the smile seemed more like a sarcastic grin.

He pressed the lion's nose and waited.

It was a different one who opened up.

She was tall and slim and was dressed in leopard-skin. Her thick auburn hair matched the color of her eyes. "Monsieur Radkin?" she asked.

He nodded.

"Entrez. Please." She had a dazzling smile. Probably straight from the dentist's, he thought.

"Where's the other one?" he asked, looking around for the Japanese woman from last time.

"Mademoiselle Yoko? But it is 'er night off." she said, ushering him into the large room with the dome.

"I see," Joseph replied.

"I am called Fifi." She tilted her head in an alluring pose. "May I offer you a drink?"

"A scotch," he said. "Make it a double."

She disappeared, perhaps not as quietly as Yoko, but quiet enough.

He walked over to the cathedral window and looked out. The moon still hung brightly in the sky. The waters below were sparkling like a commercial for Perrier. He looked slightly to his right, through the glass doors, and saw the woods.

"Beautiful on a night like this, isn't it?"

It was Saunders. He had two glasses in his hands. He handed Joseph one. "I think this is yours."

"Beauty has its price, I guess," said Joseph, taking the glass and downing some of it. "Good scotch." Has its price, too, he thought.

"Glenlivet." Saunders raised his glass. "Pure grain. No additives. No hangover."

"Yeah," said Joseph, "if everyone was rich, I guess we'd all have ocean views and forests off our deck and no hangovers."

"If everyone was rich, no one would have anything. Just between you and me, Radkin, there's not enough Glenlivet to go around."

"Or trees," said Joseph, gazing out at the forest.

"There are plenty of trees. And the nice thing about them is they always grow back."

Joseph looked at the man standing next to him. He seemed so self-assured and so at ease. A prince, he thought. In his castle on a mountain top. "Would you say the same thing about those?" he asked, motioning to the forest of eucalyptus trees.

Saunders chuckled. "You wouldn't want to spoil my view, would you, Mr Radkin?"

"I wouldn't want to spoil anybody's view, Mr Saunders." He rubbed the bandage still on his cheek. "Nor would I want to spoil anybody's face."

"That's a pretty nasty bruise," Saunders said, somewhat solicitously. "What happened to you?"

Joseph took another drink. "Don't worry about it," he said. "It was all in the line of duty."

"Well, I certainly didn't want you to get hurt," said Saunders walking over and putting his glass on the mantelpiece.

"Did you say the same thing to Armstrong? He got a little more hurt than me."

Saunders turned back to him. "Armstrong?"

"Surely you couldn't have forgotten his name already? Or is it your habit to forget about the people that you use? Let me refresh your memory. He was the insurance investigator who had looked into the McCullough lumber mill fire some years back. You hired him to do some work for you. I met him on the plane. You bought two tickets—two adjoining seats, one for each of us."

"Would you like another drink, Mr Radkin?" Saunders said, in way of reply.

Joseph emptied his glass. "Sure. Why not?"

Fifi came in. Maybe she was stationed in the hall. Maybe she had a sixth sense. Anyway, she took the empty glasses as Sanders ordered two of the same.

"Your old friend Bright told you about him, didn't he?" said Joseph, after Fifi left. "That is to say, he let you know about the information that had come into his possession. He had contacted you some time ago asking for your help. He was concerned about the new pulp mill that McCullough Industries was planning. He was upset about the dumping of dioxin . . ."

There was a whimsical look on Saunders' face. It seemed to him that the lion had one, too. "What are you getting at?" he asked.

"You two were friends. From Stanford, wasn't it? And you had access to certain information through your relationship to the magazine. Access to information and to staff." Joseph stopped a moment. "And then there was the Papyrus Club . . ." He stared at Saunders as if to gauge something.

"Please continue, Mr Radkin. I must say I'm finding this very interesting."

"You and Bright and Felix Tobias. All brilliant young

students, I suppose. Fascinated with the history of paper. You all went your separate paths—you into business, Bright to academia, Tobias into finance. You were all successful. And, one way or another, it all had to do with paper . . ."

He stopped as Fifi brought in the drinks. She handed him a glass and gave him another dazzling smile.

She left and Saunders winked. "She doesn't have anything to do with paper, Mr Radkin."

"But she's here because of what's printed on it."

Saunders made a face of mock disappointment. "You mean you don't think she likes me for my looks?"

"Insofar as you look like money, women like her probably love you for your looks. But, frankly, Mr Saunders, I don't give a shit. What I do give a shit about is being used." He took a swig of his drink. "Frankly, I don't like it!"

"You were paid well enough," said Saunders. "It was a simple assignment. You were to find out something, write down the information and send it back. No one told you to lie or to make anything up. You just presented me with the facts. Is that what you call being used?"

"Let's stop playing games, Mr Saunders, OK? You found out about McCullough's troubles. Bright wanted to stop him from building the pulp mill, but you wanted something else. You contacted Tobias. The King of Arbitrage. He could smell a way to make a fortune. And it had to do with what you all loved. So you devised a game plan. You knew McCullough was vulnerable. But vulnerability is nothing without maximum exposure. And that exposure had to be perfectly timed to influence the stock market. So you hired two people. Armstrong—because he had been on McCullough's case before and he could smoke him out. And me—because you needed a reporter who would be picked up by the wires. Someone you had leverage over. Someone who could be trusted . . ."

Saunders walked over to the glass doors that led to the deck and opened them up. "So you think it was all about money, do you?"

"I did," said Joseph, following his movements with his eyes. "But now I know it's more . . ."

Saunders smiled. He motioned to the trees. "They're very beautiful, aren't they? And I love protecting beautiful things."

"It's ironic, isn't it?" said Joseph. "You saved your trees and destroyed a forest. All for the want of a view!"

"But what a view!" said Saunders. "What a magnificent view! And he would have had them all cut down!"

"Those uneconomic trees finally had some value, didn't they? I didn't piece it all together until I found out who owned that land across there."

"They had tried to get the cutting rights," said Saunders. "I couldn't understand why. Why would anyone want to buy a forest of useless trees?"

"And then you found out about the Brazilian ship. If McCullough's tests had been successful, they would have used your precious eucalyptus trees, wouldn't they? I mean why continue to import logs from Brazil if you can get them from a neighboring state?"

"Of course." Saunders was still gazing up into the hills. "They would have all been cut away."

"Instead, you had Bear Creek cut to finance your acquisition."

"I'm truly sorry about that," said Saunders, "but it couldn't have been helped."

Joseph ran his fingers through his hair. "What really gets me," he said, "is that McCullough was actually going to build a pulp mill that would have been clean. Those eucalyptus trees don't need to be bleached. So there wouldn't have been spill-offs of dioxin. Now you have your fucking view, but the rivers will continue to be polluted and one of the last of the ancient forests has been cut down."

Fifi came in carrying some towels. "I take a hot tub now, OK?" She smiled seductively at Joseph. "Will Monsieur Radkin come, too?"

Saunders looked at Joseph and narrowed his eyes. "No, my dear. I don't think Mr Radkin is going to stay."

Chapter 25

It was about one in the morning when he got home. Polly was still awake.

"Look at your face!" she said. "You look awful! Is that what happened to you in Oregon?"

"Yeah, but you should see what happened to them."

They went into the kitchen. She fixed him a drink and he told her all about it from beginning to end.

When he was through, she said, "One thing I don't understand. That man Armstrong. Why was he acting like your personal 'Deep Throat'?"

"Armstrong was the investigator for the insurance company that wrote the policy on McCullough's lumber mill. When it burned down, he was sent to investigate—that's standard procedure. He had strong suspicions that arson was involved— strong enough for payment to be held up. But he could never prove anything.

"After Bright told Saunders about the evidence McCullough's daughter had given him, Saunders traced Armstrong down and hired him to reopen the case on Haveck and McCullough. The way Saunders figured it, seeing Armstrong around again would put extra pressure on them . . ."

"But wouldn't it put them on their guard?" she asked.

"It didn't matter," he replied. "Saunders just wanted to turn up the heat. Of course Saunders knew about the diary. Though Bright never told him where it was hidden. I assume Armstrong was searching for it when Haveck got to him . . .'

"But why did he come to you?"

"Saunders wanted to put me on the trail of the Brazilian ship and make it appear that I discovered it myself. That was

Armstrong's other job. To lure me in. But Armstrong wasn't as dumb as he came off. In fact, he was a pretty decent man. He found out what Saunders was up to and passed me the message by sending the card for the Park Lane Hotel. Somehow he took a liking to me, I guess—I don't know why. Maybe I'm just a likeable guy—or maybe I reminded him of his kid. Anyway, after he got shot, he came to warn me. He didn't like being used any more than I did . . ."

She caught the look in his eye. She reached out and took his hand. "Don't be too down on yourself, Joseph," she said. "McCullough was an evil man . . ."

"Who did some good things," Joseph reminded her. "He was trying to run a clean shop. He agreed to save the forest . . ."

"Temporarily," she said.

"Life is only temporary," he replied. "So then there's Saunders who's a decent man—so to speak. He gives his money to liberal causes. He helps fund *Investigations Magazine*. And because of him the forest is cut down, shipped off to Japan and a lot of pulp mill workers in Oregon will be looking for a job."

"That's not your fault," she said.

"I was a part of it," he replied, looking into her eyes.

"In that case a bank clerk who accepts money from the Mafia is complicit in trafficking cocaine."

"You know it's not the same thing," he said.

She sighed. "You can't always be correct, Joseph."

"I don't mind not being correct," he replied. "I just don't like feeling so dirty."

She got up from her chair and walked behind him. She got an envelope from the cabinet where they threw the mail and put it on the table by his hand.

"This came by special messenger today."

He opened it up. It was a check made out to him from Saunders.

"My second payment," he said. "Blood money."

She was still standing behind him. She put her arms around his neck and said, "I love you, Joseph. I'll respect any decision you make."

181

"How much do we have in the bank?"

"Not much. But we'll manage. We always have."

"Let me think about it," he said.

"Fine," she replied. "Let's sleep on it."

"I can't go to sleep yet." He looked down at his glass.

She gave him a kiss on his wounded cheek. "Goodnight," she said, "I'm going to bed."

He finished half a bottle of whisky that night. He kept staring at the check and ended up falling asleep in his chair.

It was a strange, drunken dream that he had. But when he woke up, very early in the morning, before the cry of the first babe or the scream of Polly's alarm, he knew what had to be done.

He had thrown on his jacket and was hurrying out when Polly called to him.

"Joseph! For goodness sake! Where are you going so early?"

He came into the bedroom, looking like the loser in a barroom brawl. "I had a dream last night," he said. "A vision."

She rubbed her eyes and yawned. "Don't tell me you've found religion, Joseph. I've lived with you too long for you to spring that on me now . . ."

"No," he said, "it's nothing like that. There's just some things I have to do."

She glanced at the alarm clock. "Now? It's six o'clock in the morning!"

"Yeah," he said, "I know. But it's so crazy that if I don't start on it I won't and then I might regret it later."

"That doesn't make sense," she said, pulling up the covers and throwing them over her head.

"It has to do with the thing that came in the mail yesterday . . .'

"Go ahead and do what you have to do, Joseph."

"You don't mind?"

"It's your check."

"Will you be home later?" he added as a postscript before going off.

"I'll be home. I was hoping you'd spend the day with me and the kids."

"I will," he promised. "I just have a few more things and then I'll be done."

He walked around on the beach getting it all straight in his head. When he finished thinking it out, he drove over to the Insta-Print shop just as it was opening.

Rossi, the guy who ran the place gave him a quick lesson in using the desktop publishing device.

"You can lay out anything you want," said Rossi, going over the instructions with him. "You have access to thirty different kinds of type."

Joseph spent an hour programming in the story and setting it up. When he was finished, he sat for a while admiring it.

"So you going into business for yourself?" asked Rossi, helping him do up a copy.

"It's just a one-time thing," said Joseph.

"That's what they all say. You want I should print it up for you? How many?"

"How many can you do for a thousand bucks?"

Rossi raised his eyebrows. "For a thousand bucks? Pretty many!"

He told Rossi he'd pick them up that evening. Then he walked down the block to a certain store.

"What kind did you want?" asked the skinny shop keeper.

Joseph described what he wanted again.

The shop keeper stuck a finger in his ear and gave it a twist. "I never heard of one like that. Not a pedigree, at any rate. I can't think of where you'd find it, unless . . ."

"Unless what?" asked Joseph.

"Well, you might just try the pound."

It was a few hours later that Joseph came back home. In his hands he held a box.

"Whatcha got in there, hotshot?" asked Polly coming over for a look.

"Something for the kids," he said. "Where are they?"

"They got bored waiting for you. They're upstairs with your

mother." She stared at the box as it shook. "There's something live in there," she said. She glanced up at him.

He looked back at her sheepishly. "Yes, there is."

"What is it?"

"Remember when I told you about that dog last night?"

"You mean the one who saved your life?"

"Yes. Ludwig." He scratched the back of his head a little nervously. "Well, he was part of my dream."

Her foot was tapping the floor, rhythmically. She did not look pleased. "Who's going to feed it?" she asked. "Who's going to take it on walks? Who's going to clean up its shit?"

It wasn't euphoric happiness he saw in her eyes.

"OK, Polly, I'll take it back."

She made a face. "Well, let's take a look at it, at least."

He opened up the box. She looked inside.

"That's a dog?" she asked.

"Yes."

"But it's so tiny! It looks more like a mouse."

"It's a dog. Really. I got it at the pound. They wouldn't put a mouse in the pound, would they?"

"I guess you're right," she said.

"It's amazing," he said. "It looks just like him."

"Ludwig? The dog who saved your life looked like that?"

He nodded.

She put her finger in the box and touched its nose. It stared up at her and made a woofing sound.

"It likes you," said Joseph.

She looked at him. "How do you know?"

"I can tell."

She touched its nose again and it licked her finger with a slurp. "I guess it wouldn't eat much," she said.

"In fact they told me at the pound that it probably would survive on a bowl of pabulum and an occasional bone."

"Something that small wouldn't make too much of a mess, would it?"

"How could it?" asked Joseph. "I mean it probably would find a corner and lie in it all day and night."

"It does have cute ears," said Polly. Then, looking up at him she asked, "Is that what you spent your three thousand dollars on?"

"Not quite," he said, pulling out of his pocket a copy of the broadside he made. He unfolded it and showed it to her.

"'*Midnight Special*'," she read. "Nice name." She looked back at him. "So you became a dog owner and publisher all in one day."

"You have to own a dog if you're going to be a publisher," he said. "It's an obligation."

Polly glanced through the copy. "Pretty emotive stuff," she said. "I guess this will ruffle a few feathers . . ." She gave him a certain look. "If anyone gets a chance to read it, that is."

"Oh, they'll read it all right," said Joseph.

"They might read it, but you have to get it to them first, champ."

He put a finger to his head and winked. "I've thought of that," he said.

It was late at night after he had picked up the boxes of the *Midnight Special* that he drove down to the tiny airport in Santa Clara.

Tony was waiting on the runway standing next to his two-seater Piper Cub as Joseph drove up.

"I don't like this, man," Tony said as he took a carton of papers from the trunk after Joseph got out and opened it.

"I thought you said you did this before." Joseph lifted another carton out and handed it on.

"Yeah. In the sixties. Man, that was light years ago. Back then I did a lot of crazy stuff! Now I'm a legitimate businessman!"

"Don't gripe," said Joseph. "You're making damn good money. More than you probably make hauling the marijuana crop down from Humboldt County."

"Whoa!" Tony lifted another box and loaded it on the plane. "How do you know how much money I make? Besides, flyin' hash you don't get caught. Droppin' leaflets, you're nothin' but a clay pigeon."

"That's why we're doing it at night!" said Joseph, handing the final carton on.

"Well let's see what I'll be droppin', at least." Tony tore open a box and took out one of the broadsides. He glanced through it. "Yeah," he said, nodding his head, "it's a shame about clear cutting them old growth forests. They're doing it up where I am too. We're bein' sold down the river to a bunch of greedy bastards." He looked back at Joseph. "That'll be a thousand smackers. Cash on the barrel."

"Too bad more people can't be legitimate businessmen like you," said Joseph, handing him an envelope of money. "How do I get in?"

He had to admit it was beautiful up there in the sky. Up with the moon and the stars. It gave him a feeling of enormous freedom and energy. The very opposite of his reaction the first time he travelled up to Oregon.

It was a quick two-hour trip. They followed the coast line to Astoria and then turned right, trailing the Columbia till they saw the towers of downtown Portland come into view.

The Piper Cub glided quietly over the city and then swooped down as Tony sent hundreds of papers fluttering to earth.

"The guy who wrote that manifesto about the forests—what's his name?" Tony asked as he brought the plane into a steep ascent.

"Wolenski."

"Yeah. Who is he?"

The plane swooped down again and they made their dump.

"A very curious person," Joseph said.

"I guess," said Tony, bringing the Piper back into a climb. "You sure went to a lot of trouble over him."

"It's sort of a memorial," said Joseph.

"We got one more carton to memorialize. Which side of the river do you want it?"

"This one's special. It goes back to the San Francisco area," he said.

They flew back down the coast till they were about twenty miles north of the Golden Gate Bridge. He told Tony to fly low enough to see the landmarks on the ground.

When he found the spot he wanted, Joseph pointed down.

186

"Do me a favor," he said, "buzz that house. I think it's laughing at us."

"Sure thing, man," said Tony, sending the plane into a dive. "I hate houses that laugh."

A handful of broadsides floated onto the deck. A few straying into the sauna bath.

The rest of them sailed silently like tiny missiles into the forest, becoming seditious ornaments on a thousand eucalyptus trees.

At the end of the manifesto was a quote which read:

"Today we are just hundreds and you will have our forest. But the earth is angry and the skies are growing dark. Tomorrow thousands will replace us for they see where you have led. And the next day will come millions."

The name he signed was "Tara".